THE
VENGEANCE
BRAND

Other books by Michael Senuta:

Incident at Copper Creek

THE VENGEANCE BRAND

•

Michael Senuta

AVALON BOOKS
NEW YORK

Published by Thomas Bouregy & Co., Inc.
160 Madison Avenue, New York, NY 10016

Library of Congress Cataloging-in-Publication Data

Senuta, Michael.
    The vengeance brand / Michael Senuta.
        p. cm.
    ISBN 978-0-8034-9820-4 (acid-free paper)
    I. Title.

    PS3569.E63V46 2007
    813'.54—dc22

                                    2006034818

PRINTED IN THE UNITED STATES OF AMERICA
ON ACID-FREE PAPER
BY HADDON CRAFTSMEN, BLOOMSBURG, PENNSYLVANIA

To those who rode tall in the saddle and entertained
me for so many years in literature and on the screen

Chapter One

Brad Connors adjusted the patch over his left eye before he left the mercantile.

It still felt awkward on his face despite the fact that he had worn it for better than eight months now. He thought he might never become inured to the idea that a circular piece of leather could supplant that part of his face where his eye had once been attached.

Nevertheless, it had been the opinion of the Army surgeon that his eye had been so severely damaged that there was no alternative. A lengthy diagnosis showed that an irreparably impaired optic nerve, severe skin lacerations, and a shattered cheekbone had sealed his fate and added him to the list of those combatants who would forever remain disfigured.

It was not as though his looks had ever been anything at which to marvel. At best, he had always been a plain man with a face that looked like a weathered oaken bucket. Still, a man took pride in what the Lord had given him and held, deep inside, a bitterness for that which diminished his original composition. Added to

1

his now scarred face was a short, stubby body—barely
five-foot-six—that appeared to perch precariously on a
pair of bowlegs.

Once, he had been described as a fence post with the
knots in all the wrong places.

Such an appraisal seemed accurate to him, and he
had long ago settled into a comfortable niche so far as
his appearance went. Now, however, his modest expec-
tation of his looks had fallen even farther.

He descended the two steps that took him from the
boardwalk to the dirt street and strode to a buckboard,
strategically positioned in the shade of an elm. In the
rear among a small mountain of supplies, sat Tim
Dugger, his thick coat bundled about him despite the
warm temperature. His eyes stared vacantly at something far away. The lad, barely eighteen, had been
through some kind of hell, and Connors wondered if
the young corporal would ever recover. Somehow he
doubted it as he climbed onto the seat of the buckboard
and sat next to a tall, thin man who held the reins loosely in his sun-browned hands.

"That's it, Captain. We're packed and all paid up."

Captain John Waverly nodded as he glanced around
at the collection of clapboard structures that looked as
though they had been thrown together overnight.
Without speaking, he slapped the reins against the
horse, a sturdy chestnut with white stockings on its
forelegs, and the wagon jolted forward.

The men rode in silence for several minutes until
they reached the outskirts of town. Here, they were met
by the final member of their party, a man on horseback
who looked as though he belonged in the saddle. He
was bronzed by the sun, had broad shoulders, and a
sturdy trunk. The only blemish to his otherwise perfect

physique was a shirtsleeve that was folded in half and pinned at a place where his left elbow would normally have been.

In spite of the loss of his limb, Lieutenant Dell Chandler still carried himself with the same self-assurance he displayed on the battlefield, an assurance that had so often inspired those about him to distinguish themselves in the line of fire.

Chandler established eye contact with Waverly and Connors and then, without an exchange of words, fell in behind the buckboard at an easy gait.

For hours they rode on in relative silence, taking in the lay of the land, each man alone with his own thoughts, sometimes lost in a deep reverie. Only the occasional jerk of a wheel entering a rut or striking a rock reminded them of their present state of being and returned them to an awareness that they were still alive and held some significance in the scheme of life.

At noon, they called a halt and made camp near a small stream in a grove of aspens. Connors and Dugger gathered wood and made a fire. Chandler watered the horses while Waverly brewed coffee and fried some bacon. Biscuits and cold ham complemented the meal as they sat around the fire and chatted sparingly, mostly about the beauty of the spot.

Connors noticed that Waverly was massaging his leg. The captain grimaced at times but did not cry out.

"You all right, Captain?"

Waverly nodded. "Just a little stiff is all. I guess I'll have to get used to it."

"It'll probably give you more trouble when it rains."

"That's what the surgeon said. Dampness and cold will more than likely wreak havoc with it."

"Knew a man once back in Ohio who could tell the

weather by the rheumatism in his knee. In fact, he came to be the most accurate weather forecaster in the county. Used to make bets on it. Won a pile of money doing it. Folks even held contests pitting him against others who claimed they had the same skill. Why, I remember once he was matched up against a gent from out of state who had quite a reputation himself. His rheumatism was in his shoulder."

"What happened?" Dugger asked.

Connors took a swallow of coffee. "Well, people gathered from miles around, made bets and everything. Thousands of dollars were at stake, just to see which one of 'em was more accurate. The event took place in a barn on the farm of one of our neighbors. That's where the two squared off."

"How can you wager on a thing like that?" Chandler asked as he bit into his last piece of bacon.

"People wager on anything. It's just human nature, I guess. I had a quarter eagle on the local man myself."

"Did you win?" Dugger asked, his attention focused closely on Connors, as it so often was.

Connors frowned. "Not exactly."

"What's that supposed to mean?" Chandler inquired.

"Well, the local man predicted rain. The gent from out of state called for snow. Everybody placed a bet on his favorite and waited. The truth of the matter is that it didn't rain or snow. Clouds formed, the sky grew dark, and it started to sleet."

Waverly shook his head.

"There was some argument over whose prediction came closer. One camp declared that sleet was nothing more than frozen rain and that their man should be proclaimed the winner. The other side judged that the word 'frozen' more accurately described snow rather than rain. A heated debate broke out, and a fistfight even erupted."

"How was it finally settled?" Dugger queried eagerly.

"Well, a bolt of lightning struck the barn, and it started to go up in flames. Everybody helped in forming a bucket brigade and, between the falling sleet and our efforts, we managed to put out the fire with a minimum of damage to part of the loft. The contest was declared a draw, and every man walked away with the same number of coins in his pocket that he started out with."

Waverly stood up, stretched his stiff leg, and limped toward the buckboard.

Chandler rolled his eyes as he tossed the last of his coffee from his cup.

"Yeah, I guess it's about time we traveled," Connors put in, grinning at Dugger.

Dugger smiled as he replayed Connors' story in his mind.

The men broke camp and were soon back on the road.

An hour later they encountered the first people since starting their journey. A covered wagon approached them pulled by a pair of worn-looking horses. A man of about fifty held the reins. Next to him was a frail woman in a faded bonnet and a calico dress. They drew up alongside the buckboard and came to a halt.

"Howdy," the man said, flashing a friendly smile.

"Hello," Waverly replied, touching the brim of his Stetson and nodding to the woman.

"Where're you bound for?"

"California," Waverly replied.

"That's quite a venture."

"We figure it should take us close to three months," Connors returned, "but we aren't in any hurry."

"The wife and I are on our way back from our spread in Oklahoma. Didn't fare that well. Got word that my uncle up and died back in Indiana. Left us a bootmaking business. Don't know much about boots, but I'm fixin' to learn. I reckon it can't be any worse than tryin' to raise crops that don't want to grow. On the way back, we thought we'd visit some friends in these parts."

"We wish you the best," Waverly returned.

The man focused his attention on Connors and then on Chandler. His smile faded. "You boys look like you did some fightin'."

"We did a bit," Connors replied.

"Union?"

"The Twelfth Ohio Cavalry," Connors said.

The man exchanged a look with his wife and then forced a smile. "Well, we wish you well too." He slapped the reins to his horses and pulled past the buckboard.

Chandler touched the brim of his Stetson as they moved by his horse.

"Seem like decent enough folks," Waverly said as he started the horse.

"Yeah," Connors said as he touched his eye patch. "I guess it's going to take some getting used to."

"What's that?"

"People staring at you like you're some kind of freak."

Waverly frowned. "Most people who have never been in combat don't have any idea what it involves. They understand the attraction of soldiering, the trappings—brass buttons, gleaming sabers, blaring bugles . . . but the actual experience of being in battle . . . the sweating, the bleeding, the dying . . . well, that's a different thing. The scars of war aren't as pretty to people as shiny boots and colorful uniforms. They take some getting used to—both for those who carry them and for those who have to look at them."

"I imagine so," Connors replied, pulling his Stetson down more tightly as he stared off into the distance.

They made good time for their first day of travel and camped not far off the road at the base of a rocky overhang. A trickle of water from a deep fissure in a boulder gathered into a pool and was more than enough to satisfy their needs for the evening.

Chandler removed his saddle and blanket and picketed his horse nearby. It was a dun-colored mare, swift enough, and alert to the sights and sounds around her. She was a good buy, Chandler thought, as he rubbed her ears and ran his hand down her thick mane. Next, he unhitched the chestnut and picketed it close to the mare. It was also a dependable animal. It took direction well and worked with a steadiness that made the price he had paid for it a steal. A solid judge of horseflesh, he had once considered going into the business of raising horses, but the war, among other things, had altered his plans. Now, with the loss of his arm, he had conflicting feelings about his future.

Dugger gathered wood for the fire and unpacked the bedrolls from the buckboard.

Waverly and Connors prepared a tasty dinner of beans, bacon, and coffee. Canned peaches served as dessert.

The men worked together with an almost mechanical precision, their military training dictating their individual responsibilities as they moved about camp, complementing one another with an efficiency that reflected their years of discipline and familiarity with each other. Few words were necessary as each man knew and executed his unwritten tasks.

The conversation was light but limited following the meal as each man found his bedroll in his own good time and drifted off to sleep. Chandler was the last to retire, for his mind was unsettled. He removed a letter from his shirt pocket and read it over and over, as though attempting to discern a meaning that lay beyond the written words. He was unsuccessful in doing so and concluded his efforts by folding the document and returning it to his pocket. In time, his mind could no longer concentrate, and he lay back on his bedroll and succumbed to fatigue.

Waverly was the first to stir. He had slept well once the pain in his stiff leg had subsided. Now, he could feel it again—a dull, throbbing ache like a tooth that needed to be extracted. He sat up on his blanket and rubbed his leg vigorously. Sometimes the stimulation from his fingers alleviated the discomfort; sometimes he had to live with it. After several minutes, he decided that this was going to be one of those mornings he was going to have to live with the pain.

He stood, stretched his limbs, and then made his way to the pool of water. He drank several handfuls. The water was clear and tasted fresh. He then located his razor and mirror from his kit on the buckboard and went to work.

A few minutes later, he studied his reflection and saw a man that he barely recognized. His face was thin, and tiny wrinkles had formed around his eyes. His hair, though still thick, had flecks of gray.

He had come a long way since his early days as an officer. He remembered a time when he had been young, exuberant, and even a touch haughty. The exuberance had remained with him for many years, but the haughtiness had dissolved quickly as he grew to recognize and appreciate the value of most men who wore the uniform. Soldiering was a hard life. Few men became rich at it. Advancement was difficult. Most complained about the conditions, the duties, the inconveniences. There were even the occasional malcontents, but by and large, most men he came to know were fine, stable individuals who acknowledged the importance of their training, followed their orders to the best of their abilities, and were ready to lay down their lives for the cause in which they believed.

It was hard to harbor feelings of superiority when one fought beside such individuals. As Waverly tempered his outlook, those men who came to know and follow him grew to honor and respect him. Few men in the Union Army were held in such regard by their comrades in arms.

Now, he had reached a crossroads in his life. His injury and state of mind were such that he could no longer serve his country in the capacity of a soldier. The war was over, and he knew he had seen his last campaign. He was tired—of fighting, death, and destruction. It was time now for the nation to heal and for those who had fought and struggled for so long and hard to heal their minds and bodies.

He knew that he could never forget the past, but it was important for him not to dwell on it. He could not allow the past to destroy what was left of him. There had to be a safe haven somewhere on the road ahead where he and his companions could find peace and lead productive lives in their remaining years.

As he glanced at the slumbering figures by the fire, he knew how the passions of the past had affected the lot of them. The boy, Tim Dugger, in particular, had lost the most, for he was the youngest and the most severely injured. When Waverly thought about the years remaining for each of them, he shivered when he considered Tim.

Waverly tossed several more sticks on the fire. He then filled the coffeepot and began to brew the grains. He placed a slab of bacon in the frying pan and watched the meat as it began to shrivel. He enjoyed the aroma and delighted in hearing the bacon sizzle in the pan. There would be no more life or death confrontations for him, no more strategies to plot, no battle plans. From now on, he would take pleasure in the simple things in life—trout fishing in a quiet stream, preparing a meal, sitting in a rocking chair and watching the sunset.

The savory smells of the bacon and coffee commingled with the wood smoke from the fire and wafted over the camp. The others began to stir. Soon, they all had a plate before them and were enjoying their first meal of the day.

Always a voracious eater, Connors vigorously attacked the food and downed three cups of coffee before he slowed down. "Never knew that you were this handy with a skillet, Captain. I've got a strong feeling that the officers in the unit should've done the cooking."

"Yeah, that's for sure," Dugger added. "The last cook we had burned everything—potatoes, beans, beef . . . even the coffee."

"Glad you like it," Waverly replied. "Beans and bacon seem to go together as well as any combination I can think of."

"I heartily agree," Chandler put in. "I always did like beans for breakfast."

"Always better on the second day too," Connors added.

"That's true enough," Dugger said with a grin.

"Some foods just naturally taste better on the second day, but there's something about a plate of reheated beans that can't be beat," Connors returned.

"The juices have to have time to meld together," Waverly explained.

"Never knew a soldier who disliked beans. I guess though when you add a strip or two of bacon to the mix, you just have a marriage that will satisfy most any man," Connors philosophized as he lifted a huge forkful from his plate and downed it with pleasure.

"Do you figure those Rebs enjoyed beans as much as us Yanks?" Dugger mused.

"Most of them were more than likely partial to goobers," Connors said with a wink.

"Don't let him fool you, Tim. Most any man would favor a menu that featured beans. It's my guess that no man would turn them down," Chandler replied.

"The Southerners are good cooks, that's for certain," Waverly offered. "I spent some time in the South in my younger days. Some of the cooks, as I recall, used a touch of Tabasco sauce as a flavoring in some of their bean dishes."

"My mother used to use molasses," Connors returned.

"I heard that down around the border they're partial to chili peppers," Chandler added.

"Some of those Mexican cooks put chili peppers into just about everything," Connors said as he stood and patted his stomach.

"I had some prepared that way once," Waverly said, placing his cup on a rock and standing. "The peppers surely do get a man's attention, but I always thought they took away the basic flavor of the beans."

Connors grinned. "When you get older and your taste buds begin to go, hot peppers liven things up for you."

"Maybe we should buy some for you when we reach the next town," Waverly said with a smile.

Dugger chuckled as he regarded Connors.

"What are you laughing at, old-timer?" Connors asked.

Dugger laughed out loud.

The others were glad to see the sight, for there had been few moments of contentment for the lad since his injury. Their mood was light as they concluded their discussion and then went about breaking camp. Dugger filled the canteens and then helped Waverly with the cooking utensils. Connors harnessed the horse to the buckboard, and Chandler saddled his mount. In no time they were under way again. The ground was level and the road smooth. They made good progress, although they were in no particular hurry. The sky had few clouds, and the sun shone brightly against a dusty blue backdrop. It was the kind of day that made a man feel positive about himself and his future.

Waverly lost himself in his surroundings, content at this stage of his life to appreciate the small things he had not found time to enjoy since he was a boy back on the Ohio River. He recalled, for instance, how he had loved to fish. He was a bit amazed that he had not had a pole in his hands since he had entered the Army some ten years ago. He wondered where the time had gone and how he had allowed his lifestyle to change him so much that he had not taken pleasure in some of the simple pursuits he had enjoyed the most.

Connors harbored similar sentiments. He, too, enjoyed the landscape. In particular, he had always been an admirer of trees—big trees, stately trees—and there were many oaks to be seen. They were strong and tall, with thick branches that reached out in every direction.

He recalled an oak he used to climb as a youngster. He marveled to himself about that special time in his life when climbing an oak tree was about the best thing in the world for a boy to do. Why, he wondered, did men not climb trees? Was it because they were too busy, too concerned with life around them, too self-conscious that others would laugh at them? He thought about all the occasions when he just wanted to walk up to a big tree and climb it.

Once, in the heat of battle, he noticed a solitary oak in the middle of a pasture. There were troops all around it, firing at each other, trying to gain an advantage, killing and being killed over a plot of ground in which no farmer would be likely to show an interest. During a lull in that skirmish, Connors remembered taking a swill of water from his canteen and pausing to stare at that tree. He considered how much more pleasant life would be if all the combatants would stop trying to kill each other long enough for him to climb that tree. When the firing resumed, however, he was startled out of his reverie, and he realized that that phase of his life—and probably the life of everyone on that field of battle—had passed by. More than likely, he would never climb another tree, but he would admire them, and he would remember the times when he did. Maybe, he might even carve his initials in one.

* * *

It was mid morning when Waverly brought the buckboard to a sudden halt. Connors jerked forward, and Dugger slammed into the back of the seat.

"What is it, Captain?" Connors asked, staring at Waverly.

Scanning the terrain ahead, Waverly replied, "I thought I saw movement in those bushes."

Connors focused on the area in question, a thick cluster of brush about a hundred yards ahead, just off to the right of the road. He saw nothing.

Chandler brought his horse up alongside the buckboard and glanced down at Waverly, who pointed toward the brush.

Dugger had turned around and was on his knees, facing the road and the brush.

For a full minute, they remained frozen in their positions, alert to the lay of the land before them. Ruled now by training and field experience, each man gauged distances and assessed the terrain for cover and concealment should an attack prove imminent.

Finally, Waverly conceded, "Maybe I was wrong. It might have been the breeze rustling the leaves."

Connors did not respond, his attention still riveted on the brush.

It was then that the mare's ears pricked up, and the chestnut nickered softly.

Connors turned and held out his hand. In what was no more than a second, Dugger had placed a Henry in it. Connors leaped from the buckboard and started for a thick tree some twenty yards off to the left. When he reached it, he levered a cartridge into the chamber and took up a defensive position.

Waverly signaled to Chandler, who circled his horse wide to the right of the brush. He loosened the thong on his .44. He then reached under his coat and reassured himself that his backup .44 was tucked under his belt at the small of his back. Working with one arm now, he no longer carried a rifle. It was too cumbersome and too awkward. A .44 Colt was now his principal means of defense. Even reloading a handgun with one appendage proved difficult and slow. That was the reason he carried a spare. A matter of seconds in returning fire could be the difference between life and death. Reassured of his firearms, Chandler made a slow, deliberate circle to the right of the brush, his hand holding his reins loosely, ready to move toward his holster at any given moment.

Waverly handed the reins to Dugger and stepped down slowly. He moved to the rear of the buckboard, located his saddlebags, and pulled out his .44, which he held loosely in his right hand, pointing the muzzle toward the ground.

Another two minutes passed before they saw a branch move. A pair of eyes appeared from among the leaves, and then a sudden movement advertised the presence of a buck springing from his cover and darting off toward another cluster of brush further away.

Connors lowered his Henry and grinned as he strolled back toward the buckboard.

Chandler approached from the opposite side of the road, pulled up next to Waverly, and smiled. "Looks like our Rebel friends have grown some antlers, Captain."

Waverly relaxed and smiled back. "I guess I'm still a little jumpy."

Connors tossed his Henry back to Dugger, who caught it and replaced it on the bed of the buckboard. "Your senses are still refined, Captain. You're alert."

"Yeah. I just hope that I'm not so alert that I shoot a

Michael Senuta

drunk coming out of a dark alley or open up on a child playing in the bushes," he returned, hanging his head.

"You can take off your uniform, but it takes a while to burn the soldiering out of a man," Connors replied.

Waverly nodded, tucked the Colt under his belt, and then climbed back on the buckboard.

Chapter Two

Late in the afternoon, they reached a small town called Caleb. The livery was the first building they saw. It was a dilapidated structure with a peeling sign over the door that read LOGAN'S. A man of about sixty emerged to greet them. He had a bulbous nose and a ragged beard. He wore a battered hat, red suspenders over a faded shirt, and pants that were worn at the knees.

"Would you be Mr. Logan?" Waverly asked.

"At your service," he replied.

"Can you stable our horses for the night?"

"Sure can. I've got several empty stalls at the moment."

"Give them plenty of oats."

"They'll never eat better. You want me to tend to your rig as well? I can check your wheels."

"Go ahead. How much?"

He rubbed his beard as he made a mental calculation. "A dollar seventy-five."

Waverly started to reach into his pocket, but Logan waved him off. "You can pay me when you leave town."

Waverly nodded. "Is there a good hotel in town?"

"There's only one, and it's fair enough. You'll find it on the next block on your left. It's nothin' fancy, but the cafe next door has good food. It stays open until eight."

"Much obliged," Connors said as he climbed off the buckboard. "Can you keep an eye on our gear?"

"Consider it done. What about that Henry? You want me to look after it as well?"

"Do you think we'll be needing it?" Connors asked.

"Shucks no, Caleb's a peaceable community. I'll lock it up for you until you call for it."

The men selected the items they would need for a night in the hotel and left the remainder on the buckboard. They crossed the street and walked down the boardwalk toward the hotel.

Caleb was, indeed, a small town—three blocks and one main street. The hotel was called The Grand. It was anything but. The building needed paint, and the overly small lobby contained a collection of faded divans and armchairs.

The desk clerk was a small bespectacled man with a starched white collar and a frayed blue suit. He seemed the perfect complement to his surroundings. He eyed them suspiciously at first and was obviously taken aback by Connors' eye patch and Chandler's empty sleeve. However, he did his best to overcome his mild shock at their appearance and offered them what he described as the hotel's best rooms. Connors, for one, appreciated the clerk's effort to act natural.

"Do you have baths available?" Waverly asked.

"We do. A bath will cost you an extra two bits."

"It'll be worth it," Chandler replied.

"Do you want to take your baths now?"

"As soon as possible."

"I'll have the boy start on your water right away," the clerk said as he handed over two keys.

They climbed the stairs to the second floor, where they located a pair of rooms opposite each other at the end of the hall. Waverly and Chandler took the one facing the street while Connors and Dugger took the one that overlooked an enclosed yard in the rear of the hotel. They were a pair of small rooms with basic conveniences. Each had two single beds, a washstand with a bowl and a pitcher of water, a bureau, and a wooden chair. The walls were decorated with a rust-colored paper, and there were some drab-looking pictures of landscapes hanging about the rooms. Nevertheless, the linen was clean, and the hotel was quiet.

Two hours later, they had all bathed and changed into clean clothes. They strolled over to the cafe and entered a room that seemed to be too spacious for such a small town. An elderly couple sat at a table in the middle of the dining room, but all the other seats were empty. A pretty waitress of about sixteen approached them and smiled shyly.

"Are you still open for dinner?" Connors asked.

"We sure are," she beamed, concentrating her attention on Dugger, who grinned back at her sheepishly. "Sit wherever you like."

They took a large table near a window and studied a chalkboard that contained the day's specials.

"I'll take the fried chicken, mashed potatoes and gravy," Connors announced.

"I'll take the same," Dugger chimed in.

"Have you got hot biscuits?" Connors asked.

"We sure do."

"Beefsteak for me, fried potatoes, and greens," Waverly said.

"Same here," Chandler added.

"And bring a pot of coffee," Waverly added.

The waitress smiled as she made a note on her pad. She then hustled off and disappeared into the kitchen.

"Pretty girl," Connors commented.

"Yes, and she seemed to take particular interest in Tim here," Chandler returned.

"I noticed," Connors returned, grinning.

Dugger shook his head. "Aw, she was just bein' nice."

The others chuckled.

It was not long before the waitress carried out a tray laden with steaming plates of food. A mountain of biscuits and a beaker of honey presented a particularly pleasant sight. On her second trip, she carried a huge coffeepot with which she promptly filled four cups. The men eagerly dug into their dinners, concentrating on their food for several minutes before speaking.

"I like your work with a skillet, Captain, but it's good to get a home-cooked meal once in a while," Connors announced.

"Here, here!" Chandler put in.

Dugger nodded in agreement, his mouth full of chicken.

"I can't argue with any of you. This is a hearty spread," Waverly returned.

Throughout the course of the meal, the young waitress returned again and again to refill their cups and to present them with additional biscuits. The men ate to their hearts' content and began to feel completely comfortable.

After a spell, the waitress brought out an apple pie,

sliced it into four pieces, and served it. They were all more than satisfied, except for Connors, who ordered and ate a second piece before rolling up his napkin and dropping it on the table in front of him. While nursing his fourth cup of coffee, he began one of his usual discourses.

"I expect that apple pie is my favorite dessert. We used to have some apple trees on our farm back in Ohio. My brother and I would pick bushels of apples, and my mother would make tarts, jellies, pies, and even cider out of them. I liked them all, but I have to admit, pie was my favorite. My father claimed that our apple trees grew from seeds that were planted by John Chapman himself."

"Who might John Chapman be?" Dugger asked.

"Most people knew him better as Johnny Appleseed."

Dugger shrugged his shoulders.

Connors flashed a surprised look at the youngster. "Do you mean to say that you never heard of the man who traveled from state to state planting apple seeds?"

"I can't say that I have. Why did he do a thing like that?"

"So that settlers and pioneers would have apple trees along the routes they traveled. They would always have the sweet, juicy fruit of the apple to help refresh themselves as they journeyed about," Connors explained.

"Did someone pay him to do it?"

"No, he was just a kind person who spent his life helping others."

"Seems like kind of a strange way to spend your life," Dugger said. "How did he make a living?"

"Some say he owned his own orchard. Did right well by it too. Didn't you read about him in school?"

Dugger frowned. "I only had five years of formal schoolin'. After that, my aunt and uncle, who took me in after my folks died, took sick and passed on themselves. From then on, I was in an orphanage for two years, and then left to work on a farm. I worked near every day. There wasn't much time for books. After that, I joined the Army."

"You lied about your age, I understand?" Waverly said.

"Yes, sir, I did."

"Why would you want to join up at such a young age? Didn't you know there was a war going on?" Chandler asked.

"Well, sir, I didn't much feel like I belonged on the farm. Oh, I wasn't mistreated or anything, but I just wasn't one of the family. I was only a worker. I never really had anybody since the age of ten. I never felt important—not since my folks died anyway—but I figured that in the Army, I could at least be a part of something important. I read in the newspapers those speeches that Abraham Lincoln made, and I listened to people talk about the Union, and I decided that I was a part of something after all. I was a part of the Union, and I wanted to fight for it."

The others exchanged glances, and then Chandler placed his hand on Dugger's shoulder. "You're a part of something all right, Tim. You belong. You're one of us."

The youngster beamed.

The waitress skimmed by and asked them if they wished anything else. They all shook their heads. Waverly settled the bill with her and inquired about breakfast.

"We open at seven o'clock. Best food in town," she said with a smile.

The four men left the café and returned to the hotel, where they sat down on some benches near the front door. Only a few people strolled by, and one rider passed on a smart looking sorrel. Soon, night fell, and the crickets began to chirp. A half moon hung low in the sky, spreading light over the buildings and the trees in the distance, but only for a short time, for a heavy cloud bank began to roll by. They withdrew to the lobby, where Waverly picked up a newspaper, perused it for a few minutes, and then tossed it back on the side table where he had found it.

"Anything new?" Chandler asked.

"No. The paper's a week old. Just some local gossip."

They retired for the evening.

They awoke early the next morning to find that it had rained during the night. The streets were wet and muddy, and the sky was heavily overcast. They felt a chill in the air as they made their way back to the café. It was seven sharp when they walked into the eatery. Surprisingly, it was already crowded. The pretty young waitress was not on duty. In her place was a slow-stepping waiter of about thirty. He was pleasant enough, however, and brought them—they agreed—one of the best breakfasts they ever had. Connors ate twice as many pancakes as any of the others, which he covered with a river of maple syrup. Supplemented with bacon, eggs, and a pot of coffee, each man left with a good feeling in his stomach.

They returned to the hotel for their gear, settled with the clerk, and then crossed the street to the livery. Logan saw them approach and brought out their horses. He harnessed the chestnut to the buckboard and produced the Henry, which Dugger secured with the rest of their belongings. Logan then saddled the dun.

"Fine lookin' animals you got here. Mighty gentle too."

"Dependable as well," Connors returned.

"I enjoyed doin' business with you. Stop in again if you're ever passin' this way."

Money exchanged hands, good-byes were made, and Logan waved to them as they rode down the main street and left behind the town of Caleb.

By midmorning it began to rain—lightly at first, but the menconsidered it a forewarning, and they stopped and donned their slickers. Within an hour the rain was heavy, and an occasional streak of lightning seared the sky. Thunder followed, violating the tranquility of the landscape, reminding them of cannon fire and making them uncomfortably aware of the insignificant role they played on earth. A small flock of birds hastened past them in search of a safe haven from the mounting storm. The wind began to blow, and the rain came down in oblique sheets. Soon, the moisture turned to hail, and they were pelted unmercifully as they rode on, their shoulders bowed and their Stetsons pulled low over their eyes. Chandler rode on ahead, searching the terrain for shelter. For some time, the others lost sight of him as they struggled onward, but then he suddenly appeared from out of a stretch of oaks and waved them in his direction.

Waverly turned the chestnut, and they rode toward Chandler, who waited for them for some time before spinning his mount and disappearing again into the trees. The wheels of the buckboard rolled over a span of rock-studded ground, jolting the three men severely. The chestnut, never hesitating, negotiated a descent so sheer that Dugger was nearly thrown from his perch among the gear on the back of the buckboard. However, a few additional yards brought them to a more tolerable grade that led them to the base of a vast overhang, where Chandler was standing. He motioned to them, and Waverly pulled the chestnut to a halt at his feet.

"There's a cave over here. It's even large enough to shelter the horses," Chandler shouted over the maelstrom of swirling wind and stinging hail.

Waverly and the others climbed off the buckboard. Connors quickly unharnessed the chestnut and led it toward Chandler, who was strides ahead, walking his mount between a pair of man-sized boulders into what appeared to be a cleft in the wall. Within seconds, the two horses were standing side by side, their eyes adjusting to the darkness of the cavity. Chandler returned to the buckboard to help Waverly carry what essentials were needed to camp the night, while Dugger made a quick circle through the area, gathering as many dry twigs and branches as he could carry.

Soon, the four of them were ensconced within the cave, and in no time, Dugger had a warming fire going. The flames curled smoothly over the wood he had gathered, comfortably enveloping the men in a soft circle of light. Waverly removed a long stick from the fire and held it high overhead, thereby casting a revealing glow over the extent of the cave. It was perhaps fifteen feet deep, high at the opening, but tapering down to a ceiling of no more than five feet at the rear. It was a comfortable arrangement, and Waverly felt that they were fortunate to have discovered such a location.

After peeling off their slickers, they stood near the entrance to the cave and watched the trees bend and sway in the wind. The hail continued to pummel the earth, leaving behind a blanket of white pellets the size of marbles. The chestnut nickered softly, and Chandler patted down its flank reassuringly. It craned its head, seemed to accept its situation for the moment, and then turned away again and sniffed at a tuft of grass growing at its feet.

In time, the hail alternated with the rain before it disappeared altogether, leaving a steady stream of raindrops that saturated the ground. They watched through the upper branches of the tall trees as countless streaks of lightning severed the black sky. The lightning was followed by deafening claps of thunder that seemed to shake the earth around them.

Suddenly, Dugger started to swoon. His arms began to tremble, and he fell to his knees. He covered his face with his hands as he teetered forward.

Connors caught him, preventing him from toppling onto his face. Chandler stepped forward and took hold of the youngster's arm and, between the two of them, managed to get him into a sitting position.

"Where's his medicine?" Waverly asked.

"In his shirt pocket," Chandler returned.

Connors pulled a tin from Dugger's pocket, opened it, and extracted a pill, which he placed into the young man's mouth. He then grabbed a canteen and held it to Dugger's lips.

Dugger's eyes rolled around in his head, but he managed to focus on Connors long enough to accept the water and swallow the pill. He continued to shake violently and pressed his hands to the sides of his head. Connors and Waverly wrapped a blanket around him and helped him to stretch out on the floor of the cave. His trembling continued for several more minutes as his limbs jerked spasmodically. Finally, his body movements subsided, and he closed his eyes and turned over onto his side.

"These seizures aren't good," Waverly said.

Connors shook his head. "They don't seem to happen as often, but when they do, they're mighty severe."

"The doctor explained that they could disappear completely, or they could kill him," Chandler added.

Waverly's lips tightened. "He never should've been issued a uniform. He was too young to see action."

"He fought well when he had to," Connors returned.

"He was too young—just a boy."

"It wasn't the war that did him in. It was that devil incarnate—Traxler," Connors said.

"Traxler was a part of it, but the boy should never have been in that butcher's hands to begin with," Waverly countered. He turned away and stepped back to the mouth of the cave, where he stood in silence as he watched the lightning crash through the clouds. He knelt down and picked up a stick, which he turned over in his hands again and again.

Connors and Chandler sat down on either side of the fire, respecting Waverly's desire to be alone. Connors fished out his pipe from his coat pocket and used one of the burning twigs to light it. Soon, the pleasant mixture of his tobacco blended with the smoke rising from the campfire. The cave was warm and dry, a far cry from the storm that raged around them. It was a reprieve of sorts, like a temporary escape from battle—a moment in time when life came to a halt and one was able to take stock. For a long while, the men remained where they were, standing and sitting, their eyes focused on the increasing darkness around them.

In time, the thunder ceased, and the rain fell in a

softer patter that was easy on the ears. Then, the quiet within the cave was temporarily broken when Waverly snapped the stick in two. He turned, a pained expression on his face, and dropped the pieces into the fire.

Chapter Three

The heavy rains from the previous day turned the road to mud. Waverly was bad-tempered, as they were forced to stop repeatedly to free the wheels of the buckboard. Travel was a slow, labored process, and they made less than half the distance they covered on an average day.

"This does it," Waverly finally announced after pulling his foot out of a mud bank and climbing back onto the seat. "When we get to the next town, we're going to trade in the buckboard for some horses."

"What about your leg, Captain?" Dugger asked.

"I can ride all right. It's stiff, but I won't be any worse off in the saddle than on this bogged down washboard. We can buy a pack horse for most of our gear."

Connors pulled out a map and searched their route. "Looks like a town about ten or twelve miles up ahead. We might be able to make a trade there."

"At this rate, we should be there in two days," Waverly frowned.

They moved on, struggling with each mile of road,

but progressing nonetheless. It was late afternoon when they encountered a woman seated in a buckboard in the middle of the road. Her wheels were mired deep, and it was obvious at a glance that she was not going anywhere. As they approached, she looked up, a forlorn expression on her aged face. She was a heavyset woman, wearing a faded coat, a floppy hat, and pants that were covered with mud up to her knees.

Waverly brought the buckboard to a stop about twenty feet short of her vehicle, which looked altogether like a ship that had run aground on a sandbar. Touching the brim of his Stetson, he said, "Ma'am, can we be of any assistance?"

She looked from one to the other of them as though fearful of their appearance and seemed in doubt as to how to respond. Anxiously, she pulled her coat closer about her.

Sensing her uncertainty, Connors said, "Don't be concerned, ma'am, we're just some weary veterans on the move west."

She forced a half smile. "I thank the Lord for sending someone," she said. "I've been stuck here for the better part of two hours. Didn't know what I was goin' to do."

Chandler rode up beside her buckboard and glanced down at the wheels. "You've worked your way in pretty deep, all right." He rode up to her horse, an old swayback that had seen better days. He patted the horse gently as he looked down into a pair of tired eyes.

"Old Brownie is too spent to pull anymore. I think we're in so deep now we might as well take up residence."

"We've contemplated the same situation a number of times today ourselves," Connors replied as he,

Waverly, and Dugger climbed down and moved toward her buckboard.

Waverly assessed the supplies the woman was carrying. "We can unload these sacks of feed. That should lighten the burden a bit."

"Do as you think best," the woman replied.

As Waverly and Dugger removed the sacks, Connors made his way to the front of the buckboard, where he helped Chandler unharness Brownie.

"You need a breather, old fellow," Chandler said soothingly as he led the worn-out horse off to the side of the road. He then unsaddled the dun, and they substituted her in Brownie's place.

Connors then rejoined Waverly and Dugger behind the mired buckboard, and the three of them began to push. Their joint effort, coupled with the dun's younger legs, easily dislodged the buckboard from its muddy trap. With Chandler walking beside the dun and leading her by the harness, they maneuvered the vehicle to a piece of higher ground off to the side of the road that was far less boggy. They then reloaded the supplies and returned Brownie to his harness.

"I don't know how to thank you boys," the woman said, a genuine look of relief on her face.

"No thanks needed, ma'am," Waverly returned as he wiped the mud from his hands.

"There's no need to call me ma'am. My name's Flora Hitchings."

"A pleasure. I'm John Waverly. These men are Brad Connors and Dell Chandler. The young one over there is Tim Dugger."

She smiled at each of them in turn. "You say you're veterans?"

"We are."

"Yankees, if I'm not mistaken. Not that it matters because the war's over."

"We fought on the Union side," Waverly replied.

"The reason I asked is because my late husband Tom was a veteran. He fought at Buena Vista in 'Forty-seven."

"That would be under General Taylor," Waverly noted.

"That it was. A fine man, too, according to my husband. Bless Tom's soul. He's been gone now more than ten years, but that's another matter. What can I do to repay you?"

"Your gratitude is more than enough," Connors returned.

She suddenly smiled broadly. "Why don't you boys join me for dinner. My spread is only a few miles east of here. It's nothin' fancy, but I've never had any complaints about my vittles."

"That isn't necessary, Mrs. Hitchings," Waverly said.

"Call me Flora, and I insist. A veteran is entitled to a good meal. Besides, you boys muddied yourselves up pretty good helpin' me out. The least I can do is give you some soap and water and a dry place to spend the night. My bunkhouse is a lot warmer than that fleabag of a hotel they've got in town."

Her words were friendly, and her intentions seemed genuine. Waverly glanced at the others. Chandler smiled, Dugger grinned, and Connors nodded. "All right, Flora. We accept your invitation."

She beamed. "Good. Now, you just follow me. I'll guarantee you a hot meal that you won't be forgettin' for some time."

They fell in behind her and, about twenty minutes

later, emerged into a small valley bounded by stands of tall trees. It was a pretty sight, with a stream running through a grassy meadow where a milk cow was grazing. The spread was composed of three buildings—a small farmhouse, a barn, and a third building that must have been the bunkhouse. A corral held half a dozen horses.

Flora pulled up her buckboard in front of the farmhouse and climbed down. Moving stiffly, she straightened herself out and then rubbed her lower back. "The bones are gettin' creaky. I'll surely welcome some dryer weather."

"It should be coming soon enough," Connors said, casting his eyes skyward.

"You boys give me a chance to start the meal. The pump's in front of the bunkhouse. You're welcome to store your belongin's in there. I'll give you a shout when dinner's ready."

Chandler dismounted and dropped his reins over a hitching rail. Waverly, Connors, and Dugger climbed off the buckboard and secured their gear. As they strolled toward the bunkhouse, they noticed a chicken coop near the barn, where eight or ten hens were cackling as they scratched the ground. The birds seemed to be oblivious to the men as they moved about erratically, pecking at the dirt and even at each other.

The bunkhouse looked to be a ramshackle structure. The roof needed shingling, and the paint was nearly gone. The door squeaked on its hinges as Waverly opened it and led the way in. The interior was another story, however. It was clean and tidy. There were six bunks, but only one seemed to be in use. The sole inhabitant's belongings were neatly arranged around his bunk. Some shirts hung from wall pegs, and a wooden trunk reposed at the foot of the mattress. There was a wood stove centrally positioned in the room, and a bin filled with kindling wood stood next to it. Some shelves lined with plates, tins, and sacks of sugar and flour filled one wall. A large round table was positioned near the stove. A cupboard was stocked with several bars of soap and a pile of towels. The men selected some bunks, spread out their gear, and then proceeded to wash.

About an hour later they heard Flora call to them, and they made their way to the farmhouse. The front steps were rickety, and the roof over the front porch needed some support work. The interior of the house was humble but clean. A sofa and some worn chairs were comfortably arranged around a huge stone fireplace. Some paintings of landscapes adorned the walls, and there was an old china cabinet filled with crockery against one wall. A long table was set for five, and the hearty aroma of cooked meat filled the air.

"Sit down, boys, and make yourselves comfortable," Flora announced. She had changed into a pretty calico dress. Her hair was neatly fashioned in a bun, and she looked refreshed and content.

Connors held out a chair for her, and she smiled her thanks as she sat down at the head of the table. When she was seated, the others took their chairs.

"You boys are certainly mannerly," she stated.

"A lady should always be treated with respect," Chandler replied.

Beaming, she said, "I hope you like beef stew."

"Why, it happens to be Tim's favorite," Chandler announced.

"Is that so?"

"Yes, ma'am," Dugger returned.

"Well, you boys dig in," she directed as she passed around a huge plate of cornbread.

Waverly poured himself some coffee from a formidable looking pot and then handed it to Chandler.

They found the stew hot and well seasoned. The cornbread was a perfect complement, and the coffee was strong and savory.

"One of the finest meals I've ever sat down to," Connors announced as he spread a large dollop of butter on a square of cornbread.

"Oh, you're just plain hungry. Road travel will do that to a bein'," she replied, but she was obviously pleased with Connors' remark.

"How long have you had this spread, Flora?" Waverly asked.

"Close to twenty years now. We built it from the ground up."

"You seem to have only one hand, judging from the gear in the bunkhouse," Waverly said.

"That's right. I only keep one hand now—Clem Hazeldine. He's seventy-five and beset with the rheumatism. Between the two of us, we manage to keep the spread goin'."

"Is he working the fields?" Chandler asked.

"No, he's back in Pennsylvania, tendin' his sick mother."

"His mother?" Connors asked in surprise.

"That's right. She'll be ninety-six this year. The Hazeldines are known for their longevity. Oh, she's comin' along just fine. He wrote me that he'll be returnin' real soon."

"What do you raise on your farm?" Dugger asked.

"Corn mostly. I've got a good garden of vegetables. That and a few pigs and some chickens are about all I need to get by, and gettin' by is about all I care about since Tom passed on."

"No youngsters, Flora?" Waverly inquired.

She shook her head. "Tom and I were never blessed with children. If we had been, I'd have somebody around here to care for and tend to. The truth of the matter is that the chores are all I have now, and they get mighty burdensome at times."

Waverly glanced at the others as he took a sip of coffee.

"Well, you boys have the run of the place. Help yourselves to some more vittles if you like," she said, pushing her chair away from the table. "I've got to visit the widow Nelson just up the road. The poor soul broke her arm last week when her mule took a notion to kickin' her. I promised to lend a hand with the cleanin' and such. I won't be back till mornin'." She walked to the door and threw on her coat. "I'll be sure to fix you a first-class breakfast when I get back," she said over her shoulder.

Dugger leaned back in his chair and stared out the window. "You know, Captain, that roof over the bunkhouse needs some work. I wouldn't want to get wet tonight. I think I'll see if Miss Flora has any shingles in the barn."

"While you're at it, see if you can turn up an extra hammer and a saw. The porch needs some improvement as well," Waverly replied.

"We could also use some lumber," Connors added.

Chandler pushed himself away from the table. "While the rest of you are seeing to the property, I'll tend to the stock."

They left the table and headed for the door but not before Connors took another piece of cornbread and stuffed it into his coat pocket. For as long as they had daylight, they occupied themselves with an assortment of tasks. Each labor, in itself, was small, but the sum total would leave Flora Hitchings with a little bit more of an edge than she had on the previous day. It was late, and they were genuinely tired when they made their way back to the bunkhouse.

On the following morning, they heard Flora's rig, and they went out to meet her. Dugger helped her down and smiled when he saw her face light up with surprise as she was about to step onto the porch. Glancing around, she beamed with excitement. "What have you boys gone and done?"

"Well, Tim here decided that your bunkhouse roof needed a patch or two," Connors announced.

Flora took Dugger's face in her hands and squeezed it in delight.

"We replaced a support beam here and there on your porch, repaired your steps, and added a hand rail," Waverly added.

"Also, your wood bin was empty, and your corral needed a few nails," Chandler put in.

"Your chicken coop needed a bit of work too," Dugger said.

She pressed her hands to her mouth, and tears welled in her eyes. "You shouldn't have done all this, boys, not for me."

"Well, we figured that your place has been suffering a bit since your hand has been gone. Besides, you sacrificed doing things for yourself in order to help another who was worse off than you. Sometimes folks need a shoulder to lean on," Connors said.

"I don't know what to say," she returned, tears rolling down her cheeks.

Waverly rested his arm on the seat of her buckboard. "Tell me, Flora, we've been contemplating trading our buckboard for some horses. Chandler is as good a judge of horseflesh as anybody I know, and he says that you've got some fine looking mounts in the corral. Would you consider a swap—with some cash thrown in?"

"Cash is mighty hard to come by these days," she said. "I'd welcome any kind of a trade."

"We'll be needing two saddle horses and one to pack our supplies."

"Take your pick of the lot."

"Name your price," Waverly returned.

"Twenty apiece sound fair?"

"Well, I've got to be honest. When it comes to horses, I never argue with the lieutenant here. He tells me they'd be a bargain at thirty. Plus, we'll throw in the buckboard. We just won't be needing it anymore. It's in better shape than yours, and we'd like you to have it," Waverly noted.

"That it is," she said, assessing her own rig, "but I can't take advantage of those that would help me. You can have the horses for twenty apiece."

"Thirty is fair, and we'd be the ones taking advantage of you."

"How's that?" she asked.

"You did promise us breakfast, and Connors alone is more than likely going to eat up your profit margin in pancakes, bacon, and eggs."

She grinned broadly and waved them toward her. "Come on in. I'll start the coffee."

Connors and Chandler climbed the steps behind her while Waverly and Dugger brought up the rear. Dugger leaned close to Waverly and whispered, "The lieutenant told you that twenty was a fair price, Captain."

"Did he now?"

"That was nice of you . . . mighty nice."

"Well, what's a few dollars one way or another when it's going for a good cause?"

Dugger grinned as he fell in step with Waverly and the two of them started for the house.

Chapter Four

Three days later they crossed into Kentucky. The horses that Flora Hitchings had sold them—two chestnuts and a sorrel—proved to be more than adequate. Hardy and energetic, they adapted quickly to trail life and soon grasped their roles in the men's travel plans. The chestnuts alternated as pack animals, as Dugger took a personal liking to the sorrel and chose to ride it daily. It had not rained since the night of the lightning storm, and their muddy debacle on the road to Flora's farm was a thing of the past.

Late in the morning, they rode into their first town since leaving Tennessee—a modest looking settlement of a few dozen buildings. Hayricks were scattered in the distance on either side of a road that wound a serpentine route over a tree-lined hill. Some figures were working a field on the outskirts of town, and a handful of men were busy laying the framework for a new structure at one end of the main street. The noise from their hammers rang through the air, the first sound of

40

human activity the men heard since leaving Flora Hitchings' spread.

Waverly stopped in front of a barber shop and dismounted. "I think I'll get a shave," he said as he dropped his reins over a rail.

"I'll head over to the blacksmith. I want to check on the dun's left foreleg," Chandler announced.

"Dugger and I will pick up some supplies at the mercantile," Connors said.

The men went their separate ways as they set about completing their individual errands.

Waverly brushed some of the road dust from his clothes before stepping onto the boardwalk and entering the barber shop. It was a small shop, with the usual assortment of mugs and bottles situated on shelves around a dusty mirror. The odors of lotions and tonics, long imbued in the room, filled Waverly's nostrils as he removed his Stetson and coat and hung them on pegs.

"It'll be just a few minutes, mister," the barber stated as he continued to clip the reddish beard of an old man who was dozing in his chair.

"Take your time," Waverly returned, picking up a newspaper and sitting on a wooden chair near the window.

"Just passin' through?" the barber asked. He was a short man with dark curly hair and a fine handlebar mustache.

"Just passing through," Waverly replied.

"Where you headed?"

"California."

"California! That's quite a ride."

"That it is, but I'm in no rush."

"Got a job waitin'?"

"No. I hope to find some land there . . . settle down."

"Ranching?"

"If things work out, I wouldn't mind starting a spread," Waverly replied.

"Ranching is hard work."

"That's true enough, but I'm no stranger to long hours. Besides, I like the idea of having some ground I can call my own."

The barber nodded, a wistful look in his eyes.

Waverly glanced at the newspaper, only three days old, and read an article about Reconstruction and another about the railroad before the old-timer came to life and climbed out of the barber's chair. He seemed to notice Waverly for the first time, nodded, and then plopped a battered hat on his head and left the shop.

"You're next, sir," the barber announced as he shook out his chair cloth and brushed off the leather seat with a small broom.

Waverly moved across the floor stiffly, dragging his leg a bit, and sat in the chair. "Just a shave," he said.

Within a minute, the barber had frothed some lather in a mug and began to spread it on Waverly's face. "Ex-soldier?" he asked.

Waverly nodded.

"Union?"

Waverly nodded again, not wishing to be rude, but not particularly interested in conversing about the war either.

"I've got no problem with Northerners or Southerners, but there are plenty who do. There are hard feelin's on both sides, and I can understand why. There are some who just can't put it behind 'em."

"Sometimes it's hard to forget."

"That leg you're draggin'—did you get that in the war?" he asked, eyeing Waverly narrowly.

"Not exactly."

"What do you mean 'not exactly'?"

"It's one of those things I'm trying to forget," Waverly said, returning the barber's stare.

The barber's face twitched. "Oh, sure, I understand." He honed the razor on his strop and then began a series of light strokes down Waverly's face. "Think the winter's over with?"

"I hope so. We've had a long one," Waverly replied as he closed his eyes and leaned back in the chair.

"How would you like to live in a city, Tim?" Connors asked as he and Dugger strolled down the boardwalk.

"I'm not really sure," Dugger returned, his eyes flitting from building to building with curiosity.

"Of course, this is only a small town. It's nothing like Denver or San Francisco. There are thousands of people who live there."

"Thousands?"

"That's right. People of all walks of life. In big cities, they have hospitals and libraries and theaters."

"Theaters?"

"Places where actors and actresses dress up in costumes and stand on a stage to recite lines that famous authors have written."

Dugger shook his head. "I've never seen anything like that before."

"It's called culture, and it's a good thing to experience once in a while."

"Too many people make me nervous."

Connors chuckled. "Then, you sure enough shouldn't have joined the US Army."

"That's different. I'm a soldier."

Connors smiled. "That's true enough."

They reached a tobacco shop where Connors paused and looked into the window. "You go on ahead to the mercantile, Tim. I'm going to stock up on some pipe tobacco. I'll meet you there in a few minutes."

Dugger nodded and moved up the street to a drab looking store where brooms, axe handles, rakes, and shovels were displayed in front. As Dugger passed through the door, a bell rang over his head. He looked around at a layout of bolts of cloth, coveralls, and flannel shirts. The counter was long and busy with jars of pickles, peppermint sticks, gumdrops, and licorice— the only colorful oasis in a store that seemed devoid of excitement. Behind the counter, running from the ceiling to the floor, were rows of tins, pots and pans, kitchen gadgets, tools, and boxes of nails of various sizes. Sacks of grain were stacked everywhere, making the aisles narrow and hard to navigate.

Dugger walked up to the counter and stood there, waiting for someone to appear. Finally, a man of about sixty, with wire-rimmed spectacles and a long leather apron, emerged from a back room.

"How can I help you, young fellow?" he asked.

"I'd like a slab of bacon, a sack of beans, two pounds of coffee, and a pound of sugar," Dugger answered.

The storekeeper nodded as he wrote down Dugger's order.

"I'll also take a couple tins of peaches if you have any."

"Sure do. Peaches are good for you. I always stock plenty."

Eyeing the jars on the counter, Dugger smiled. "How much for the peppermint?"

"Two for a penny or five for two pennies."

"I guess I'll take two sticks."

"Help yourself. I'll tally it up on your bill."

Dugger's lips suddenly began to twitch, and he felt his head start to spin. His hand started to tremble, and he reached out for the counter top to steady himself.

"You all right, son?" the storekeeper asked.

Dugger nodded shakily.

A moment later he heard the bell ring, and he turned to see two men saunter in. They were in their early twenties and wore farm clothes. One of them walked up to the counter and stood right next to Dugger.

"I'll take some coffee!" he snapped.

"Be with you in a minute, Barlow. Right now I'm takin' care of this young fellow."

The man named Barlow glanced at Dugger and sneered. "Don't have time for no saddle tramp. Strangers can wait in line. Locals have the right to go first."

"It doesn't work that way, Barlow. You'll just have to wait your turn," the storekeeper stated as he began to load Dugger's supplies into a sack.

"He don't mind, do you, mister?" he said, shoving Dugger hard with his elbow.

Dugger lost his balance, fell backward, and stumbled to the floor.

Barlow and the other man started to laugh.

As Dugger climbed to his knees, his hands began to tremble wildly.

"Look at the saddle tramp, Barlow," the other man said. "He's shakin' in fear at the sight of you."

Dugger's hands moved to his face, shaking violently now as his head felt as if it were about to explode.

Barlow stepped over to Dugger, grabbed the lapels of his coat, and jerked him to his feet. "You're about the scrawniest lookin' saddle tramp I ever did see."

"He's shakin' like a leaf, Barlow."

"You let that boy alone!" the storekeeper said.

"You stay outta this, Mr. Lawson. I ain't goin' to hurt him . . . not much anyway."

Both men started to laugh out loud as Barlow spun Dugger around and shoved him hard across the room. Dugger fell to the floor, rolled over, and struck his head against a barrel. His arms and legs writhed uncontrollably, and his head jerked from side to side.

"Look at him, Grady, he looks like a snake."

The two men were laughing so uproariously that they failed to hear the bell ring over the door, nor did they notice Connors as he walked into the mercantile.

Connors took in the scene, saw the frightened storekeeper, and then regarded Barlow and Grady. Grady was standing closer to the door, and Connors took a step toward him.

"Well, what do we have here—a one eyed—"

Connors brought his right arm up in a sweeping arc, striking Grady with his open palm. The blow caught Grady squarely on the bottom of his jaw, picked him up off the floor, and deposited him onto the countertop. Barlow immediately stopped laughing. He took a step toward Connors and started to raise his arm, but Connors' left hand came around so quickly it clipped Barlow on the side of the face and rocked him backwards. Without giving Barlow a chance to recover, Connors followed with his open right hand, and then backhanded him with a returning arc. He repeated the sequence twice more before he turned again on Grady and delivered as many blows. The blows were swift, forceful, and efficiently dispensed, and left both men unconscious—Grady draped over the counter and Barlow stretched out on the floor, their faces red and their lips split and bloody.

The storekeeper looked on in stunned disbelief as Connors removed a bandanna from his pocket and wiped his hand.

"Would you get me a cup of water please?" Connors asked.

The storekeeper nodded numbly but did not move.

"The boy needs it—now," Connors directed.

The words finally seemed to register, and the storekeeper turned and disappeared into the back room.

Connors stepped over to Dugger, knelt down, and quickly located the tin of medicine that the boy kept in his pocket. Carefully, he lodged one of the pills into Dugger's mouth.

The storekeeper rushed out with a cup and handed it to Connors, who held it to Dugger's lips.

Dugger accepted it, coughed up some of the water, but managed to swallow a small amount.

"What's wrong with him?" the storekeeper asked.

"Head injury."

"Oh. Is he going to be all right?"

"Yes."

"He's still shakin'."

"It will stop in a few minutes. He just needs some time," Connors returned.

"Do you want me to go for the sheriff?"

Connors shook his head. "I think they learned their lesson."

"I suspect they did."

Connors helped Dugger to right himself and kept him propped up until his head cleared.

"Maybe I should go for a doctor."

"He'll be all right. He's coming around."

"I mean for Barlow and Grady."

Connors glanced over his shoulder at the two men. "I wouldn't bother. I was pretty easy on the both of them."

The shopkeeper rubbed his hand across his jaw as he considered the two men sprawled out in his store. "Yeah . . . I guess you could've been a lot harder."

Dugger sat slumped over in his saddle while Connors secured the supplies onto the packhorse. Waverly and Chandler stood beside them, holding the reins of their horses. Each man looked sad, pensive.

Turning toward Waverly and Chandler, Connors said in a low voice, "He's not handling it very well this time."

"Do you think those men hurt him?" Chandler asked.

"I don't think so—not physically anyway. It's just that he feels so helpless during the seizures."

"He must be made to realize that the seizures can grow even worse. There could come a time when he won't come out of one of them," Waverly said.

Connors nodded. "I think that's in the back of his mind now more than ever."

Chandler shook his head grimly. "It's a tough way to have to live each day of your life."

"All we can do is hope that things get better. Nothing lasts forever—not even pain and fear," Waverly stated. "Maybe, with the war over and the memories of Traxler's brutality fading, he can will his body to heal."

"Maybe," Connors said dubiously.

They mounted and slowly rode out of town, with Waverly in the lead, and Dugger positioned between Connors and Chandler.

Chapter Five

Later in the week, they saw the Mississippi for the first time. They sat on their horses for a long while and just stared at it. There was something inspiring about it, as though it had a purpose—a timetable of sorts—and everyone had to respect its ebb and flow. It stopped for no one, it took notice of nothing, yet it seemed to beckon as though it were the biggest and greatest horse any rider could ever have. "Get on my back," it might be saying, "and I will carry you to distant places you have never seen." Seeing it made one feel that he was a part of something big, almost as though he were a segment of history. It was something one could tell his grandchildren about.

They rode a meandering parallel to the water's edge for a mile or more before they decided to make camp for the night. At one secluded spot near the riverbank, they came upon a small boy who was busily lashing some boards together. When they were but a short distance away, he looked up from his work and stared at them curiously.

"What are you up to, partner?" Connors asked.

He hesitated as he looked from one to the other of them. He was about eight, with thickly matted blond hair, large brown eyes, and faded coveralls. "I'm buildin' a raft," he replied.

"Planning on doing some fishing?" Chandler asked.

"I'm plannin' on runnin' away."

The men smiled at each other.

Connors dismounted and stood next to the collection of boards.

The boy eyed him narrowly. "Are you a pirate?" he asked.

Connors seemed taken aback by the question, but he grinned as he remembered the patch over his eye. "No, son, I'm just an old soldier who lost his eye."

The boy grimaced as he stared hard at Connors, obviously wrestling with the concept of a man without an eye. Then, turning his attention to Chandler, he said, "Was he a soldier too?"

Connors nodded. "We all were. All of us had a mighty hard time of it."

Shaking his head, the boy said, "I sure am sorry to hear it."

Connors smiled. "Where will you go?"

"What?"

"On the raft, I mean?"

"Oh. As far away from here as I can. It doesn't much matter where."

Connors examined the rope the boy was using. "This rope is worn. It won't serve to lash these boards together."

The boy frowned. "It'll have to do until I can find a better one. One way or the other, I'll be leavin' today."

"What's the hurry?" Chandler asked.

"I've gotta save my mother. She's comin' with me."

"On the raft?" Waverly asked.

"Yes, sir."

"Save your mother from what?" Connors queried.

"From my stepfather. He's plannin' on killin' her to-night."

The men exchanged glances with each other.

"Just what do you mean by that, son?" Waverly asked as he dismounted.

"He'll be comin' home from the tavern tonight, and he'll beat my mother again. The last time he said he was goin' to kill her. I'm goin' to make sure he doesn't hurt her again. I'll have this raft built, and the two of us will run away together where he'll never find us."

Waverly ran his hand across his chin as he watched the boy return to the construction of his raft. "Does your mother know about your plan—about running away on the river, that is?"

"She said we were goin' to leave tonight on the river. I just figured I'd better get a raft ready."

"I see. Maybe we'd better talk to her about this."

"She'll be along any time now. She told me to wait for her here on the riverbank," the boy explained.

"What do you make of this, Captain?" Connors whispered as they watched the boy labor on his project.

"I don't know. He seems dead serious, doesn't he?"

Connors nodded.

About ten minutes later, a woman wearing a shawl and toting a sack approached from a path that emerged from a stand of trees. She walked briskly but paused on occasion to glance furtively over her shoulder. She hesitated for a long moment when she saw them, but she finally moved forward.

"There's my mother!" the boy said excitedly.

The woman walked up to the boy and placed her arm around his shoulder. He smiled broadly as he nestled close to her.

"Ma'am," Waverly said, touching the brim of his Stetson.

The woman, who was short and rather frail, nodded to him. "I don't believe I've seen you men around here before," she said, regarding them suspiciously.

"We're passing through . . . on our way west," Connors said.

"I see," she returned and then seemed to take a deep breath and release it.

"We just made the acquaintance of your son. He's been telling us an interesting story," Waverly remarked.

"Oh, what have you been telling these gentlemen, Chad?" the woman asked, looking down at the boy.

"I told 'em we were goin' to run away, Ma," he answered while considering her lovingly.

"He's telling you the truth. We are running away," she said.

The men looked at each other in surprise.

"On that raft?" Connors asked.

The woman glanced at the boards and rope on which the boy had been working and smiled. "No. I told Chad that we were going to go down the river, but I had hoped to book passage on a barge."

"I see. Would you like to ride with us?"

"Thank you, but no. It's only a short distance from here, and you'd best not be seen even talking to us."

"Well, in that case, we wish you the best," Waverly said. He and Connors mounted, and the four men turned their horses' heads.

Dugger maneuvered his horse close to Waverly's. "Captain, there's something wrong here. That lady is just plain scared. Can't we do something to help her and her boy?"

"It's none of our business, Tim. Besides, the lady declined our offer of assistance."

Dugger cast a troubled look at Waverly and then hung his head in thought.

They rode on in silence but not for more than a hundred yards when they heard a scream from behind. They halted in their tracks and glanced at each other. Waverly nodded. In unison, they turned their horses.

When they returned to the spot on the riverbank where they had left Chad and his mother, they saw a buggy nearby with a black horse harnessed to it. The horse was pawing the ground nervously and tossing its head from side to side. The boy was lying on the ground motionless. The woman was struggling to escape from the grip of a tall man who was viciously swinging his fist at her.

They rode up and dismounted quickly.

Upon hearing them, the man turned and faced them. He was about forty, with broad shoulders, a thick mustache, and a florid face. He wore a .44 on his hip. "Who are you? What do you want here?" His voice was harsh and belligerent.

Connors and Dugger immediately rushed to Chad's side while Waverly and Chandler stepped up to the man.

"I said . . . what do you want?" the man repeated.

"We heard the lady scream. We thought she might be in trouble," Waverly replied.

"She's in trouble all right. She's in trouble with me," the man rapped.

While he spoke, he continued to hold the woman by the arm. She was weeping openly and looked as if she were about to swoon.

"There has to be another way to handle this," Chandler said.

"This is none of your business. This woman is my wife."

"Where we come from a man doesn't treat his wife like this," Waverly said.

"Much less a boy!" Connors added.

"Get out of here!" the man snapped.

"No . . . please don't leave. Help my boy," the woman pleaded.

"I said get out . . . now!" The man almost spat the words.

"We'll be leaving, but the woman and boy will be coming with us," Waverly stated.

The man shoved the woman aside, and she fell to the ground in a faint. He opened his coat to reveal a star on his vest. "I'm Sheriff Brock. I'm the law in these parts. Now, unless you want to find yourselves in a jail cell, you'd best forget what you saw and leave."

Waverly and Chandler looked at each other in surprise.

"That's right, I'm the law," the man sneered.

"No law entitles a man to handle a woman and a boy in this fashion," Waverly returned flatly.

Brock's expression hardened, and his hand moved toward his gun, but Waverly was upon him before he could draw. Quickly, he slammed his fist into Brock's stomach, knocking the wind out of him and sending him to the ground, where he lay on his back gasping for air.

In an instant, Connors moved in and removed the .44 from Brock's holster, which he tossed into some weeds.

Waverly moved to the woman's side, where he knelt beside her and helped her into a sitting position. As he did so, her shawl fell to the ground, revealing her face and her arms. She was badly bruised. Some of the marks on her skin were recent, but others had been made some time ago.

In a moment, she came around. "I'm sorry," she muttered. "You're strangers, and I didn't want you to get involved. My husband is a dangerous man to run afoul of."

"We'll worry about that later."

"Is my boy all right? Is Chad badly hurt?" she asked, an edge of desperation in her voice.

"He looks to be a little shaken is all," Dugger said.

Connors doused the boy with water from his canteen and then brought some for the woman. She took a long draught, and her once frenzied breathing slowed to a more normal rate.

"I feared that he'd find out about us. I thought we could escape, but I was wrong. We'll never leave this county—not with him around. He has too much power. Too many people fear him."

"You're right about that, Helen. Nobody will stop me. I run this county, and what I say is the law."

They turned to see Brock on his feet, a gun in his hand.

"I always carry a spare in my boot," he said with a snarl.

"Abe . . . please!" the woman pleaded.

"Nobody defies me . . . nobody!" he shrieked as he backed up to the buggy and picked up a whip. "I'm going to punish you, Helen. You'll never leave me . . . not while I'm alive." He stepped toward them, raised the whip over his head, and brought it down in the woman's direction.

Chandler stepped in front of the woman and took the lash across his shoulder.

Infuriated, Brock raised the whip again, but as he did so, he inadvertantly struck the black horse across the face with the last few inches of the leather. The already agitated animal went berserk. It snorted wildly, tore at the ground, and then reared high overhead. Brock spun about and saw the horse strike out with its forelegs. He attempted to turn away, but it was too late as the frightened animal brought its hooves down upon Brock's head. Brock dropped to the ground like a sack of grain and never moved.

Chandler rushed to the horse's side, took hold of its harness, and spoke to it softly in an effort to soothe it. His efforts, along with the sight of Brock's lifeless form, seemed to calm the creature. Finally, Chandler led it away, walking it for some distance, allowing it to work out its frustration and its fear of Brock.

The woman buried her face in her hands for a full minute as she sat beside Waverly and sobbed. In the meantime, Chad had come around, sat up, and then crawled over to his mother on his hands and knees. When he placed his arms around her neck, she stopped crying and held him close to her.

Waverly stepped over to Brock's side and knelt down beside him. He knew immediately that the man was gone, his skull having been crushed. Returning to the woman, he touched her gently on the shoulder and said, "He won't bother you anymore."

The woman passed her hand across her face. "I'm not sorry. May the Almighty forgive me, but I'm not sorry."

Waverly nodded his understanding.

Connors and Dugger made a hasty fire and brewed some coffee. After a time, the woman became composed, and Chad fell off to sleep as he lay on a blanket beside her. They sipped coffee as they sat around the fire and talked in a solemn fashion.

"It wasn't always like this," Helen Brock explained. "In the beginning, Abe was gentle and kind. I was a widow with a small boy, and he showed great interest in both of us. He was a perfect gentleman during our courtship. It wasn't until a month or so after we took our vows that I came to realize how wrong I had been in accepting his proposal. I quickly learned that he was mean and vicious. He controlled Chad and me as if we were puppets. What I had mistaken for love had turned to domination. He took to drink and became perverse about all things. When I disagreed with him—even over the smallest of matters—he used intimidation and even force to get his way. I came to discover that he ran the county in the same way.

"I tolerated his drunkenness and even his heavy-handed tactics for a time. After all, I had taken my oath in church, and I did not take such a thing lightly. However, when he taunted my son out of pure mean-ness and laughed at the sight of seeing him run in ter-ror whenever he entered the room, I knew that I must act. My attempts to reason with him fell on deaf ears. He laughed at my pleas, enjoyed my discomfort. There came a time when we barely talked except by way of necessity. When I finally expressed my desire to leave him, he flew into a rage. He beat me. He nearly killed me that night, and if Chad had been present, I'm not certain that he wouldn't have harmed him as well. I car-ried his bruises for as long as I could, and then I couldn't tolerate him anymore." She took a sip of cof-fee as she stared into the fire.

"Couldn't you have gotten help from someone—a friend, a neighbor?" Waverly asked.

"You saw Abe—how he behaved. He was violent and hot-tempered with others as well. Most people feared him. They avoided him whenever possible, and that led to a lonely existence for Chad and me."

"Then, you decided to run away?" Connors asked.

She nodded. "It was the only way I could think of— the only way to escape. I have a cousin downriver. I wrote to her, asking if she could take us in until I could start a new life somewhere else. She answered me, agreeing to help. Somehow, however, I think that Abe got wind of my plan. Perhaps he had seen the letter, I don't know, but he had been watching me very closely as of late. I sent Chad out to this isolated spot on the river as if to play. I threw together some belongings and what money I had saved and then followed him here when I thought it was safe." She frowned. "As you can see, my plan didn't work."

Chandler picked up a stick and stoked the fire.

Connors glanced at Chad, who was sleeping peacefully.

"What will you do now—go downriver to your cousin's?" Waverly asked.

"Maybe . . . I don't know. There's no hurry anymore—now that Abe is dead. For the first time in a long while, my son and I will be able to find some peace." She considered them closely. "I never met you before, but you men have shown more courage in dealing with Abe than anyone I've known. You've also proven to be friends to Chad and me, and that's more than anyone has done in a long time. I thank you for that."

They wrapped Abe Brock's body in a blanket and placed him in the rear of the buggy. Waverly assisted

Helen into the buggy while Connors carried the still sleeping Chad and placed him next to her.

She smiled at each of them and then placed her arm around her son.

They watched as she drove off.

"Do you think they'll be all right?" Dugger asked.

"It's hard to tell," Waverly returned. "There are some things that people just have to face on their own. I'm afraid that Helen Brock will have to determine her own destiny from here on."

Chapter Six

They found a bargeman who agreed to transport them to the opposite bank. The boards creaked under the weight of the horses, and the craft seemed anything but safe, but it did the job, and they soon found themselves on Missouri soil.

Over the next few days, they passed through several small settlements. Cotton appeared to dominate the agriculture, along with some corn, and as they moved farther west, they saw more and more livestock.

It was early evening when they rode into a town called Carterville. There were banners strung over the main street and posters tacked to the sides of buildings. Small clusters of people mingled in the streets and on the boardwalk. A wooden platform had been set up on the main street, and burning torches illuminated the area around it.

"Is it Independence Day already?" Chandler asked.

"Not yet. It looks like an election campaign of sorts," Waverly replied.

"I hate politics—too many liars," Connors put in.

"Well, it's none of our concern any way you look at it. Let's just hope that they aren't so loud that they keep us from getting a good night's sleep," Waverly said.

They located the livery and were met at the door by a young ostler of about fifteen.

"Mistah Hayes ain't here. He's gettin' cleaned up for the rally, but I'll be glad to tend to your horses," he announced as though he held a position of great importance.

"What's all the activity?" Chandler asked as he turned over his horse's reins to the youngster.

"Why, the big election for mayor. The candidates are makin' speeches tonight," he explained as though everyone in the country should know about the event.

Waverly smiled as he placed a coin in the boy's hand.

"Thanks, mistah!" he returned, his face beaming with excitement.

"Is there a good hotel in town?" Connors asked as he removed the gear from his horse.

"The Emporium. It's two blocks down on the right. Clean sheets and good food in the dinin' room—apple pie for dessert tonight."

"Much obliged," Connors returned. Turning to Waverly, he said, "That's a full block away from the speaker's platform. We might get some rest after all."

As they made their way down the street, they passed a group of men who were congregating around one individual who seemed to be the center of attention. He was speaking loudly and gesturing with considerable animation. Noticing Waverly and the others, he paused in his discourse, separated himself from the group, strolled over, and blocked their path. He was a portly man—at least two hundred and fifty pounds, with fat cheeks and a thick neck. He wore a broad-brimmed Stetson, a corduroy coat, and shiny boots.

"Welcome, gentlemen . . . welcome to our fine town," he announced in a booming voice. "I'm Hiram Weatherbee, candidate for mayor."

Waverly nodded. "Mr. Weatherbee."

Assessing them closely, he said, "Veterans?"

Waverly nodded.

"Union or Confederate?"

"Does it matter anymore?"

Weatherbee grinned. "No, sir, it doesn't matter one bit. There are some towns in the state where people still hold grudges, but not Carterville. No, sir, we're completely impartial—completely."

"That's good to hear."

"Forgive and forget. That's my motto. It's time to move on." He grinned again, more broadly this time, as he seemed to scrutinize them with the eye of a rancher considering the lineage of a horse that was about to go on the auction block.

Waverly did not like him.

"Are you boys planning on staying on, or are you just passing through?"

"Just passing through," Chandler returned.

"I see. Where are you headed?"

"Drifting west," Chandler answered.

"Hmm . . . you boys wouldn't object to showing any identification, would you?"

"Are you the law?" Connors asked.

"Why, no, but—"

"Well, we'll be glad to identify ourselves to the law if we're asked, but not to anyone else."

Weatherbee's grin dissolved. "Now, let's not have any hard feelings, boys. It's just that we have an important election coming up, and we have to be careful that there are no outside agitators around who have been paid to disrupt or influence it through threats or intimidation. It wouldn't be the first time that my worthy opponent has resorted to such tactics."

"I can assure you that we don't know your opponent, and we're not in the least bit interested in your election," Waverly asserted.

"Oh, I believe you, I believe you, but we can't be too cautious. We don't want any riffraff around. We've got a respectable town, you understand."

"And who decides who the riffraff is?" Connors returned.

Taken aback, Weatherbee forced back his grin. "Boys, I think we've gotten off on the wrong foot. Anyone can tell that you're men of principle, and I want you to enjoy the hospitality of our fair community for as long as you're here." He pulled a stash of cigars from the inside of his coat and placed one in the shirt pocket of each of the men. "Compliments of Hiram Weatherbee!" he said before he turned away and rejoined the knot of men with whom he had been conversing.

"I'll bet that deep down he feels that he wasted his cigars on people who couldn't vote," Chandler observed.

"Windbag," Connors added as they headed toward the hotel.

They paid in advance for a pair of rooms, one at the rear of the building, overlooking an alley, and the other facing the main street. They washed, brushed the trail dust from their clothes, and then made their way to the dining room, a reasonably fashionable arrangement for so small a town. Three tables out of a dozen or so were occupied. They selected a large round table off in a corner, sat down, and picked up some menus. Before long, a waiter carrying a coffeepot and a tray of cups strolled over, smiled warmly, and poured them a hot, flavorful brew. He then took their orders. All of them chose steaks, baked potatoes, and greens.

A few minutes later, a tall, thin man with gray hair and a matching mustache sidled in and sat at the table next to theirs. He was about sixty, had soft watery eyes, and wore a tweed suit. He dropped his Stetson on the chair beside him and nodded to them. A moment later the same waiter appeared and took his order before disappearing into the kitchen.

"How are you folks tonight?" he asked in a gentle voice.

"We're fine, sir," Connors replied.

"I hope that all our doings don't disturb you too much. We're in the middle of an election campaign."

"We just met one of the candidates outside," Waverly returned.

He smiled. "That'd be Hiram Weatherbee. Most likely, he's goin' to win the election."

Connors frowned. "Well, I never really did hold much with politics."

The man smiled again. "Can't say that I blame you. Until a few years ago, I didn't either."

"What are the main issues in the campaign?" Waverly asked.

"Oh, the usual . . . but most of all, law and order. Mr. Weatherbee wants to bring more peace and stability to the community. I can't say that I can blame him."

"It seems to be a quiet enough town from what we've seen—politicking aside," Chandler replied.

"Oh, it is most of the time, but lately there's been a

rash of trouble. We've had a barn burning, some horses stolen, some vandalism."

"What's your sheriff doing about it?" Chandler inquired.

"He's a good man, but he can't be everywhere. It's hard to ride herd on a town that's as open as Carterville. Now that the war's over, more and more people seem to be headin' west. We get all sorts passin' through. Most of 'em are decent enough, but there's always a share of troublemakers as well."

Waverly nodded. "The country's changing; there's no doubt about it. It's growing fast, expanding west. There's gold and land to be had, and for some, like us, there's hope for a new way of life."

The man listened to Waverly's words and appeared to be lost in thought for a moment. He took a sip of coffee and then carefully placed his cup back onto his saucer as though he were handling something of great value. There was a benevolence about him that cast him in the image of one's favorite uncle. Finally, he said, "Land was the reason that brought me west nearly fifteen years ago. I had it in mind to start ranchin' in Wyoming or Montana. Never made it that far," he said, an edge of sadness in his voice.

"What stopped you?" Chandler asked.

"The missus passed on. She took sick of the fever. She struggled hard for days, but she was just too weak after the travel and trail life. I buried her here. There was no great interest on my part in travelin' any farther after that. I just settled down here on a small spread."

"Cattle?" Connors asked.

"I run a few head. I also own a share in the general store. Lately, I've even gotten into community service."

"Oh, what is it that you do?" Waverly asked.

"I'm the town mayor."

Waverly looked at the others and then considered the man more closely.

"Mayor Sam Springs . . . at your service," he said with a smile.

"You don't seem to be giving yourself much of a chance for reelection," Chandler said.

"Like I said, Weatherbee has pretty much got a lock on it. He's managed to exploit every weakness that Carterville has, and the people seem to be listening. I can't rightly say that I blame 'em." He shook his head. "Sure is strange though," he half muttered to himself.

"What's strange?" Waverly inquired.

"Oh, all the little things that have been happening lately—bad things. I guess Sheriff Barton and I are both on the way out."

The waiter brought their food, and they more or less broke off their conversation with Sam Springs while they ate. The meal was good, and the portions were hearty, and they topped off their dinner with huge slabs of apple pie. They bade good night to the mayor and left the dining room.

"They sure are different types of men—Mr. Weatherbee and Mr. Springs," Dugger offered as they strolled out onto the boardwalk and watched the crowd gathering around the speakers' platform.

"As different as night and day, I'd say," Connors replied.

"Well, that's one thing that makes politics so inter-esting," Waverly pointed out. "It's easier for the voters when the candidates are so different. Too bad though," he mused, "I'd hate to see someone like Hiram Weatherbee push out Sam Springs. Then again, if there's as much trouble around here as they claim, it might be time for a change."

"I'd rather have Mr. Springs for my mayor," Dugger replied.

Connors smiled as he slapped his hand on Dugger's shoulder. "Since we won't be staying on in Carterville, and since we won't be voting, I guess when it comes down to it, it's really none of our business."

After a time, they made their way into the hotel lobby, where they sat down and chatted for a while. The chairs were comfortable, and there was a shelf of books for the guests' pleasure. Chandler found one that he began to browse through, and Waverly picked up the town newspaper. Connors lit his pipe while Dugger sat in a chair near the window, from which he watched the goings on outside. A few minutes later, Dugger stood up and announced, "I think I'll go up to the room. I can get a better view of the platform and the crowd from there."

"Kind of interested in this shindig, are you?" Connors asked.

Dugger shrugged.

"Maybe some day you'll consider entering politics yourself," Connors suggested.

Dugger blushed. "Aw, I can't go around makin' speeches and such."

"Oh, you never know. At least you've got somethin' to say once in a while. I've heard plenty of speeches in my time when the speakers had nothin' to say."

"It takes an astute man to be able to stand in front of a crowd and talk for any length of time without saying anything," Waverly put in.

"Amen to that, and I'd say that Hiram Weatherbee fits that bill," Connors added.

Before long they heard a voice announcing the evening's debate. Hiram Weatherbee was introduced first, and soon the booming voice of the mayoral candidate could be heard as he began his spiel. He confidently outlined his qualifications for office and then proceeded to attack the present administration by enumerating its shortcomings, with special emphasis on the deteriorating state of law and order in the community.

"I swear . . . I've never seen a man who looked like, talked like, and acted like a politician more than that man," Connors observed.

"He's a real beauty, all right," Chandler said.

Following Weatherbee's lengthy speech, someone started to bang on a drum, and a round of cheers went up.

"I wonder how long this is going to go on?" Chandler asked.

"I think I'll go up and bury my head under a pillow," Connors said as he tapped out his pipe and placed it in his coat pocket. He climbed the stairs and entered the room he shared with Dugger. He found Dugger sitting on a chair positioned in front of the window. Connors strolled over and stood beside him, glancing out at the street below. "You've got a bird's eye view from up here, Tim."

"Sure do, and I just saw something mighty peculiar."

"What's that?"

"You see that man over there in that black shirt and black Stetson—the one just to the right of the speakers' platform?"

Connors looked carefully. "Yes. What about him?"

"Well, I just saw him come out of the side door of the express office. He was wearing a coat—a black coat. He looked around, kind of skittish like, and then sidled across the street and went down the alley here. Nobody seemed to notice him with the speech goin' on and the crowd millin' around."

"But you did."

Dugger nodded. "He took off his coat and folded it real neat. He took a packet of some kind out from under his belt and wrapped it in his coat. Then, after he made sure there was nobody watchin', he put the coat in that bin in the alley down there under some chunks of wood."

Connors listened intently. "Did he see you?"

"No, but I sure enough saw him. I was right above him the whole time. I practically could've reached down and touched him."

"Then what?"

"He strolled out to the main street and eased his way into the crowd. What do you think it all means?"

"I don't know, but it's none of our business."

For several more minutes the drum continued to pound and people shouted in the street. Finally, the scene settled down, and Sam Springs climbed the platform, where he was introduced. Springs was anything but a public speaker. His words came out slowly and awkwardly, and he was barely audible at times. He lacked the swagger and presence of Hiram Weatherbee, but he spoke from the heart and pledged to do his best for the town. There was some muted applause when he concluded, but it was obvious from the reception that Weatherbee had won the day.

As the townspeople milled about, discussing the candidates' presentations, a shout suddenly erupted from the far side of the street. It was the kind of shout that distanced itself from the election banter that was filling the air; it was, instead, a shout that signalled trouble. It was evident in the timbre of the voice and the desperate nature of the person's cry.

Many eyes turned at once to see a man emerging from the front door of the express office. He wore armbands and a shade on his head. He held his hand just over his ear as he stumbled off the boardwalk and onto the street. "The express office has been robbed . . ." he managed to blurt out as several members of the crowd swarmed around him and tried to prevent him from falling.

There were some gasps from the townspeople, followed by angry comments, and then a summons for the sheriff.

Connors and Dugger stared at each other before turning their attention to the street once again.

The clerk was helped away as Weatherbee and half a dozen others rushed into the express office. A man wearing a sheriff's star soon arrived and attempted to make his way through the crowd of onlookers. No one seemed to leave the street as people mingled around in small groups, talking among themselves, expressing their concern and anger.

"Another robbery!" one said.

"Something has to be done," another pointed out.

"Weatherbee's right," a man announced, and a chorus of voices quickly echoed his remark.

Dugger and Connors spotted Sam Springs, standing apart from the crowd, a concerned expression on his face.

A few minutes later, the sheriff and Weatherbee left the express office.

"I've been robbed!" Weatherbee announced. "They got over four thousand dollars."

A shock wave seemed to surge through the crowd, followed by angry comments from some directed toward the sheriff. Demands for action were leveled at the mayor; one individual even suggested that the James Gang was involved in the robbery. The sheriff parted the crowd as he made his way down the street, with Weatherbee following in a huff.

"Keep your eye on that woodbin. I'll brief Captain Waverly and the lieutenant," Connors directed as he turned for the door.

"Right, Sarge," Dugger replied as he leaned closer to the window.

An hour and a half later, Sheriff Barton was standing next to Dugger, staring out into the alley. He was about fifty and five-foot-six. He had sloped shoulders and a mild way about him for a lawman. Waverly and Chandler were seated on the other side of the room. Darkness enveloped them, except for a small glow emanating from a kerosene lamp that rested on a side table. The main street was relatively quiet. The crowd had lingered for some time, conversing excitedly about the events of the day before finally dispersing, leaving the street empty of any activity save for a few pedestrians and an occasional buggy.

"Yes, sir, this is the most excitement Carterville has ever had before in one day," Sheriff Barton stated, his voice barely above a whisper.

"Mayor Springs gave us the distinct impression that this was a quiet town," Chandler returned, keeping his voice low as well.

"It was until a few months ago. Then, everything changed."

"The townsmen seemed pretty riled," Dugger noted.

"That they are, son; most of 'em with me. The law often gets blamed for trouble that can't get fixed. You see, the law's visible," Barton explained.

"Weatherbee was fit to be tied," Waverly commented.

"Yeah, it was all I could do to get away from him. If you heard the speech he made tonight, you should've heard the one he delivered in the jailhouse. He wanted me to organize a posse right away. I was finally able to convince him that we couldn't do any tracking until morning."

"He owns the express office as I understand," Waverly pointed out.

"He does, and as far as that goes, I can appreciate his concern."

"What was the express clerk able to tell you?" Chandler asked.

Barton shook his head. "Not much. He said that there was one man as far as he could tell and that he must've entered through the side door, although he thought the side door was locked. Unfortunately, he only caught a glimpse of the intruder before he was struck over the head. The thief wore a bandanna over his face, and his Stetson was pulled low over his eyes. I'm afraid that this young man here may be our only witness," he explained, nodding at Dugger.

"Do you recognize the man, based on Dugger's description?" Waverly asked.

Barton shrugged. "It could be half a dozen men. I've got a pretty good idea, but I don't want to prejudice myself before I get all the facts."

"But why did the man hide the money—if it was the money—in the first place? Why didn't he just leave town?" Dugger inquired.

"He might've felt that it was too risky to be carryin' it about. Maybe he thought it would be safer to stash it and return for it later. A cunning man might just handle it that way."

Dugger nodded. "I guess that makes sense, but if I would've had the money in my hands, I sure wouldn't have hidden it. I would've made a run for it."

"I might've done the same, son, but there is, of course, another possibility."

"What's that?"

Barton started to speak, but he hesitated as he suddenly stiffened and stepped away from the window. After pausing, he said, "Are you boys familiar with the old saying . . . 'Don't curse the darkness . . . light a candle.'? Well, I do believe I'm about to light a candle."

Waverly and Chandler rose to their feet and crossed the room, where they stood on either side of the window.

"You say your friend Connors is a capable individual?" Barton asked.

"As capable as any man I've known," Waverly replied.

"Good. Then, he and my deputy should be able to do the job. I do believe that someone is entering the alley."

They heard a footfall below the window. A long moment passed, and then the figure of a man stepped into the mouth of the alley and made its way to the woodbin. He hesitated, turned from side to side, and then opened the bin and removed something. In an instant, Connors and Barton's deputy converged on him. There was a brief scuffle, but he was quickly subdued.

Five minutes later Sheriff Barton was standing in the middle of his jailhouse, flanked by his deputy and Connors. Waverly, Chandler, and Dugger stood just apart from the others while Weatherbee sat in a chair, facing Barton. Weatherbee's face was pale, his hands moved nervously up and down his thighs as his eyes leaped from one man to another.

"What exactly do you have to say for yourself, Mr. Weatherbee?" Barton asked in a gentle voice.

Weatherbee passed his hand across his chin as he tried to force a smile. "Look, Sheriff, it was all just a joke—nothing more. Nobody got hurt."

"Nobody but your clerk, who has a knot on his head the size of an egg," Barton countered.

"I'll make it up to him," Weatherbee said, a tone of desperation in his voice. "Besides, it was supposed to be only a light tap on the head."

"And that makes it all right, does it?"

"You really can't charge me with anything. After all, it was my money that was taken from my express office. There's no crime in that."

Barton frowned. "You're pretty clever, aren't you? Except that I have no doubt that you would've kept the money and still filed an insurance claim against the loss, and that happens to be fraud."

"No, no, Sheriff. I wasn't planning on doing that. I swear it! And you can't prove otherwise."

Barton considered Weatherbee for a long moment. "Maybe I can, and maybe I can't. That'll be up to the judge. But a man in your position would look mighty foolish and suspicious if he didn't file a claim."

Weatherbee started to speak but changed his mind.

"Furthermore, you pulled this stunt at just the right moment. After you delivered a speech to the whole town on the lack of law and order, you arranged for a robbery to take place. It was perfect timing—for you, and the worst for Sam Springs and for me."

Weatherbee's brow began to bead with sweat. "Look, Sheriff, it was a dirty trick, I admit, but that's the way politics is played."

"You know, I've had an uneasy feelin' about you for some time now—too many strange goings on around here—all designed to make Springs and me look bad."

"Oh, now look, Barton . . . I never—"

"Who was it that you sent to rob the express office?" Barton asked. "Was it Lem Hill?"

Weatherbee licked his lips.

"Was Hill your choice to replace me as sheriff if you were to get elected?"

"Barton, you can't—"

Suddenly, and to everyone's surprise, Barton reached out and slapped Weatherbee across the face. It was not a hard blow but a ringing one that sent a shock through Weatherbee, who touched his cheek with trembling fingers as he stared at Barton in disbelief.

"Why, you fool! This boy here saw the man that came out of the express office. He saw him hide the money in the woodbin. I can march Hill in here and have him identified in a minute if he's the one," Barton pointed out in words that seemed to level Weatherbee.

Weatherbee hung his head and then slowly nodded. "It was Hill," he announced resignedly.

"And just how many other things did Hill do on your orders . . . burn down the Petersons' barn . . . rustle cattle from the Circle Y?"

"Now wait a minute, Sheriff. I'm not admitting to any of that."

"You don't have to, Weatherbee. I've got a feeling that Lem Hill will do a lot of talkin' as soon as I lay the cards on the table. I always considered him to be a bit of a lame horse anyway. I imagine he'll spill his guts a plenty—enough to put the both of you away for a while."

Weatherbee opened his mouth as if to speak, but no words came out.

"Deputy, lock up Mr. Weatherbee here and then pick up Lem Hill," Barton directed.

The deputy followed Barton's instructions.

After Weatherbee had been placed in a cell, Barton took a deep breath and then let it out slowly. "You know," he said, "the air feels cleaner in here already. It's too late to buy you boys a drink. How about a cup of coffee?"

"Sounds good, Sheriff," Waverly said, and the others nodded their heads in agreement.

Barton distributed some metal cups and then proceeded to fill them from a charred old pot.

As they all enjoyed the steaming coffee, Barton leaned against his desk and looked around his office. "I've got to tell you, I didn't figure on holdin' down this job much longer. I've got a feeling now though that I'm goin' to be around a while."

"Glad to hear it," Connors returned with a grin.

"Yeah, we didn't like that man from the first time we saw him," Dugger added.

"He was a tad shifty," Chandler said.

"He's a politician. I don't like politicians," Connors declared. "They're a breed unto themselves."

"Someone's got to serve the people," Barton said.

"That's true, but there's a difference between serving the people and serving yourself," Connors explained.

"You make a good point, Mr. Connors," Sheriff Barton said.

"You certainly do. I never knew you to be so philosophical. Maybe you should consider campaigning for public office yourself," Waverly said with a grin.

The others laughed as Connors shook his head. "That's something you'll never see, Captain."

Chapter Seven

Dugger awoke to the sound of a thrush singing off in the distance. The sun's rays were breaking through the branches of the overhanging trees, and the morning air smelled fresh and clean. He threw off his blanket and sat up for a moment, taking in the lay of the camp. The others were still asleep in their bedrolls. The horses stood nearby, motionless, yet alert to any untoward activity. Dugger rose, dropped a few more sticks on the fire, and then picked his way down a small embankment to a stream. He scooped up a few handfuls of water into his mouth. It was cool and clean and washed down his throat smoothly. He wandered upstream for a bit until he found a large rock on the water's edge. Here, he sat down and made himself comfortable as he studied the nature of the stream. It ran a meandering path, creating gentle turns in the ground as it wound its way downhill toward some distant place he would likely never see. There were thousands of pebbles scattered along the streambed, made smooth by the constant flow of water. An occasional leaf floated by, and once he saw a small twig, tumbling and turning in the current as it enjoyed a free ride in the water. Dugger wondered if there were any fish in the stream. He imagined that there must be—perhaps some trout. He thought about returning to camp for his fishing line. It would be nice to have fresh trout for breakfast. The others would enjoy it as well. It was a lazy time for him, however. The others would probably not awaken for a while, and he had leisure minutes to think about it some more. For the time being, he just wanted to sit in the quiet of the morning and enjoy the scene.

Several minutes passed. Dugger was lost in thought as he stared almost blindly into the water. He was suddenly and unexpectedly aroused from his mood, however, when a shower of water fell upon him. He looked upward but saw only clear sky. Puzzled, he glanced down at his clothes only to find that they were, indeed, wet. He had not imagined it. As he turned, he was overwhelmed by the sight of a huge gray mass standing only a few feet from him. Startled, he rose to his feet and started to back away, but he stumbled and fell into the stream, depositing himself on his backside.

"Don't be afraid." The voice came from the nearby bank. "Jojo won't hurt you. He only wants to play."

Once again, Dugger was showered with water. Now, he was nearly completely drenched as he sat in water up to his waist. Although he had never seen anything like Jojo before in person, he had seen pictures in books that he remembered. He knew that he was staring face to face with an elephant.

Jojo immersed his trunk into the stream, raised it high in the air, and showered Dugger with water once again.

"Now, Jojo, that's enough. See what you've done to this poor man."

Jojo seemed to hang his head in remorse as he swayed from side to side.

The man was small—almost tiny compared to Jojo—as he stood beside the massive creature and patted his flank. He wore colorful clothes—a shirt with intricate stitchery, a fancy vest, and shiny boots that came up to his knees. "I'm Billy . . . Billy Coppersmith. I'm awful sorry if Jojo caused you any fright. He just likes to play, is all."

Dugger grinned, a bit relieved after his initial scare, amazed to be staring at an elephant, and amused by the unorthodox sight he imagined he must be as he sat in the middle of the stream, water running through his pants. He pulled himself out of the stream and made his way to the bank. "I'm Tim Dugger," he said.

Billy extended his hand, and Dugger took it.

Billy was about twenty, had curly blond hair, and a nice smile. "I'm sure sorry about your clothes."

"Oh, don't worry about it. A little water never hurt anybody."

"What are you doin' out here in the middle of nowhere?"

"I'm camped just a short piece downstream. My friends and I are travelin' west . . . on our way to California."

"California! I may see you out there some day. I'm with the circus. We're camped just north of here," he said, jerking his thumb over his shoulder. "We started in Chicago, and we're workin' our way west too. We must've played at least fifty towns so far. Our next big stop is St. Louis. Mr. Brando—he's the big boss—is plannin' on stayin' there for at least a week. Should pull in quite a gate."

"I sure didn't expect to see any elephants out here," Dugger said. "He's a big one!"

"Oh, he's still growin'."

"How much do you figure he weighs?"

"Better than nine hundred pounds."

"Holy—"

"He eats like there's no tomorrow."

As they spoke, Jojo's trunk reached out and wrapped around Dugger's arm. It was an affectionate caress, almost gentle, considering the enormous size of the creature.

"He likes you, Tim. That's his way of showing that he wants to be your friend."

"He sure is a lot to like," Dugger returned as he patted Jojo's trunk.

Billy reached into his pocket and pulled out a handful of peanuts. "Here . . . offer him some of these. He loves 'em."

Dugger took the peanuts and held them in his open palm. Jojo eyed them, waved his fanlike ears, and then accepted them with the tip of his trunk. He placed them in his mouth and seemed to show his pleasure by nodding his head.

"Now you're a friend for life. Elephants never forget."

Dugger grinned. "He sure is impressive. Is he the star of your circus?"

"He's one of 'em. We've also got lions, tigers, and monkeys. But for my money, Jojo's the star. I'm his trainer . . . well, assistant trainer to be exact. Mr. Squires is the official trainer, but I'm learning from him, and some day I'll be the man in charge."

"It sure sounds exciting," Dugger said, recognizing Billy's deep sense of pride.

"It's the greatest life there is! I get to work with the animals, travel, see different towns, meet all kinds of interesting people."

Dugger shook his head. "I always wanted to see the circus. Maybe I can see yours."

"Do you mean to say that you've never been to the circus?"

"I can't say that I have."

"Well, where have you been? What have you been doin' that you've never seen the circus?"

Dugger frowned. "I've been in the war."

Billy's jovial smile dissolved. "Oh. I'm sorry. You seem to be too young to have been a soldier."

"I enlisted early."

"Was it bad?"

Dugger nodded. "My friends and I were hurt pretty bad. After the war was over, we were all sick for quite a while. We decided to stick together and help each other as best we could. Wherever we go and whatever happens to us, we figure we'll be there for one another."

"That's a good way. Circus people are like that too. We look out for each other. We also look out for the animals, and the animals look out for us."

"How do you mean?"

"Well, a month or so ago, some of the rigging from our big tent collapsed and fell onto one of our acrobats. We had a devil of a time moving it until Mr. Squires got the idea of having Jojo do the heavy lifting that five men couldn't do. Jojo moved the rigging like it was no more than a toothpick. He saved our acrobat's life, sure enough. Yes, sir, Jojo is a real hero."

Dugger stepped closer to Jojo and marveled at his size. "Exactly where does Jojo come from?"

"All the way from India. His original master was a prince."

"A prince?"

"Yeah. Real rich too. They say he's got more jewels than there are cattle in the Chicago stockyards."

"Jojo doesn't sound much like an Indian name."

"It isn't. His real name is something I can't even pronounce. It comes from some city in India."

"He sure is something. Besides peanuts, what does he eat to get so big?"

"Hay mostly, and he drinks a lot of water. That's why we have to camp near lakes and streams. It's easier to lead him to water than to haul buckets back and forth."

"Captain Waverly and my other friends would enjoy seein' Jojo. How about bringin' him over to our camp?"

"Why, I'd be glad to. Jojo will even give you and your friends a free performance. You'd be surprised at the tricks he can do. He's—" Billy was interrupted by what sounded like a horn coming from somewhere off in the distance. He turned around and looked behind him. "Oh oh! They're callin' me. It's time for us to pull out. Mr. Brando is goin' to be sore at me for allowin' Jojo to get away. One rule of the circus is never to delay the progress of the caravan. I'll have to be goin'. It sure was nice to meet you, Tim."

"But, Billy . . . can't you stay for just a few minutes?"

"Sorry. I have to get Jojo back." He paused, reached inside his shirt, and pulled out a pendant that hung from a silver chain. Mounted in the center, was a huge red stone that sparkled in the sunlight. "This is one of the rare rubies from Jojo's master back in India. If you wear it around your neck, it's supposed to bring you good luck. Maybe it'll make up for you gettin' your clothes all wet."

Dugger stared at it in awe as he turned the stone in his hand. "But, Billy, I can't take your good luck charm."

Billy winked at Dugger and then turned away hastily. He used some words by means of direction that Dugger did not understand, and Jojo spun about and began to lumber away in an obedient fashion. Dugger watched them as they climbed up the rise. Billy turned and waved before he disappeared from view.

Dugger shook his head and glanced at the pendant—the only tangible reminder of his encounter with Billy and Jojo—that and his wet clothes.

The others were rising as he strolled back into camp.

Connors eyed him curiously. "What happened to you, Tim? Did you fall into the stream?"

"Actually, Sarge, I was scared by an elephant, and I sort of backed in," Dugger explained as he began rummaging through his saddlebags for some dry clothes.

"Scared by an elephant?" Chandler asked as he rose from his bedroll and stretched. "You must've had a bad dream."

"No, Lieutenant, honest. The elephant wandered off from a circus that's camped not far from here. I even met his trainer, Billy Coppersmith." As Dugger proceeded to relate the story of his meeting with Jojo, the others listened intently while they cleared the morning aches from their joints.

"That's quite a tale, Tim," Waverly said. "Why didn't you bring the elephant back to camp?"

"Well, I asked Billy to bring him here, but his caravan was getting ready to pull out."

"Are you sure the elephant wasn't pink?" Connors asked, grinning broadly.

"Aw, Sarge, you don't believe me, do you?"

"Well, after all, Tim . . . an elephant out here in the middle of nowhere . . ." Chandler said.

"Oh, yeah? Well, look at this," Dugger declared, holding up the pendant. "Billy gave it to me. He said it came from a prince—all the way from India."

The others gathered around. Waverly picked it up and turned it over in his hands.

Connors rubbed his hand across his chin.

"Billy said it was a ruby. It must be worth hundreds . . . maybe thousands of dollars."

Waverly smiled. "I doubt that it's all that valuable, Tim. It's probably more of a good luck charm."

"That's exactly what Billy said!"

"You can keep it and show it off once in a while as a reminder of your encounter with the elephant. You might even give it to a pretty girl some day as a token of your admiration for her."

Dugger beamed. "Why, I think I'll do just that. I'll wear it around my neck as a good luck charm. Yes, sir, I'll wear it wherever I go."

Chapter Eight

Two days later, Dugger began to feel poorly. They made an early camp not far off the road, near a deadfall, where a small creek gathered into a pool before disappearing into a cluster of boulders nearby. They picketed their horses, gathered wood, and started a fire. Connors opened Dugger's blanket roll, and the young man, who could hardly hold up his head, stumbled toward it. Waverly and Chandler quickly assisted, and before long, Dugger was stretched out, covered, and lost to his surroundings.

The men worked in silence, each concerned about Dugger. Before long, the food was ready, and they sat around the fire, speaking quietly, and only when necessary. It was a somber meal, mixed with thoughts of comrades who had perished or had gone their own ways after the war. The casualties their unit had suffered had been great, and the memories of many of those who had survived would forever be scarred, as were their bodies. The men agreed that it would be wise for each of them to take shifts at remaining awake—not so much for security as to maintain a vigil over Dugger should he require anything. As they finished their coffee, they discussed the feasibility of continuing west. Despite his medicine, Dugger was not showing signs of improvement. In fact, in some regards, he was getting worse. Perhaps the travel itself was too much for him. Under the circumstances, California might prove to be out of the question. They were in the midst of their discussion when they heard shots. In an instant, they were on their feet, and their hands were on their weapons. They listened intently for additional sounds. None came.

"Pistol shots," Waverly said.

Chandler nodded.

"From the north . . . and not far off," Connors added.

"We'd better have a look. Connors, stay with Dugger. Chandler and I will go."

Connors nodded as he glanced over at Dugger, who was still in a deep slumber. Waverly and Chandler saddled their horses and mounted. As they made their way back to the road, Connors pulled the Henry from its scabbard. He sat on a rock not far from where Dugger lay and rested the rifle across his knees.

Waverly and Chandler moved ahead slowly, cautiously, with their hands near their .44s, alert to any movement or noise ahead. The land was quiet, the only sound was the soft padding of their horses' hooves on the hard dirt road. It was not long, however, before they heard the harsh voice of a man, followed by the scream of a woman.

Waverly and Chandler exchanged a look and then urged their horses forward.

A matter of moments brought them to a clearing just off the road. The moon was nearly full, and there was enough light to reveal a scene that shocked Waverly and Chandler. A freight wagon was positioned under the overhanging branch of a huge elm. A man whose hands were bound behind him was standing in the wagon bed, a noose draped around his neck and slung over the branch of the elm. A man stood at the head of the wagon, a few feet from one of the horses harnessed to it. Two more men were some ten feet away, positioned on either side of a woman, restraining her arms as she struggled to free herself. Three horses were tied to some brush nearby.

As Waverly and Chandler approached, the men turned in surprise and eyed them warily. Hardcases, they wore clothes that were little better than rags. After a long pause, one of the men standing beside the woman took a step forward and glared at Waverly and Chandler. He was tall and rangy, with a rumpled Stetson and a ragged beard.

"You boys had best be movin' on. This here is no concern o' yours," he stated.

"Please . . ." the woman pleaded as she continued to struggle in the grip of the other man beside her. "These men intend to rob and kill us. Help us, please!" Her words were desperate, her voice strident, and her face was strained with fear.

Waverly rested his hand on his saddle horn, only inches from the .44 under his belt. Chandler dropped his reins and let his hand drift slowly toward his holster.

"She's lyin'! This here wagon belongs to us. It's them that tried to steal it," the same man replied.

"After you hang this man, do you plan to hang the woman as well?" Waverly asked.

The three men exchanged glances before the one, who was apparently the leader, said, "We just might at that."

The woman looked at him in terror and then struggled in vain to free herself from the other man, who held her firmly.

"Since we don't know exactly who's telling the truth, we'll be glad to accompany you to the nearest sheriff. Then, the lot of you can argue it out according to law," Waverly returned.

"You won't be accompanyin' us anywhere. We set out to hang this thief, and that's what we're goin' to do . . . and if you get in our way, you may get more than you bargained for."

Waverly did not respond, but he nudged his horse closer to the wagon. Chandler, simultaneously, turned his mount so that he was facing the other two men head on.

The leader pointed at the man standing beside the wagon. "Jubal, you whip up that horse right now! I want to see that thief dance in the air."

"I wouldn't do that," Waverly said flatly.

The man called Jubal turned and stared narrowly at Waverly and then raised his whip hand.

"It's getting dark, and I might miss the noose with my first shot, but I can guarantee that I won't miss you with my second, Jubal," Waverly said.

There was something in Waverly's words and the cool manner in which they were delivered that caused Jubal's hand to freeze in midair.

"Jubal . . . I said whip that horse!"

"I can't, Stem. He's got the drop on me. Besides, I don't have a gun."

"There's only two of 'em, Jubal, and this one's got only one arm. There's three of us. Me and Reeve will see to 'em."

"Then, go ahead and see to 'em, Stem," Jubal returned.

"Yes, go ahead and make your play, Stem," Chandler said, eyeing the man closely, "but I feel that it's only fair to warn you that—one arm or not—I can take you and Reeve quite easily." Chandler's voice had a tone to it that made his words equally as chilling as Waverly's. Furthermore, there was an ease and self-confidence in his manner that could not go unnoticed.

Stem and Reeve glanced at each other and then stared back at Chandler.

Chandler knew that they were calculating their odds, and he further reasoned that they were not the kind of men who banked on an uncertainty.

Finally, Stem moved away from the woman and held his hand far away from his gun belt. Reeve followed suit.

"Over here, miss, behind us," Waverly directed.

The woman obeyed, running quickly toward Waverly.

"Now, Jubal, suppose you drop that whip, climb onto that wagon very carefully so as not to startle those horses, and remove the noose from his neck," Waverly ordered.

Jubal did as Waverly said, and after he removed the noose, he untied the man's hands.

The man lost no time in climbing down from the wagon and stepping toward Waverly's horse, where he and the woman embraced one another.

"Now, you boys mount up and ride away, and if you contemplate doubling back, we won't think twice about shooting you on sight," Waverly directed.

Stem glared at Waverly for a long moment and then

strode angrily toward the three horses. The others followed. They mounted and rode off down the road.

Waverly turned to Chandler, who nodded and followed after them.

The woman suddenly burst into tears as the man held her closely, comforting her as best he could.

Waverly dismounted, removed his canteen, and offered it to the man. The man accepted it and let the woman drink from it. It seemed to calm her as she held her hand to her mouth and then wiped her eyes with her fingers.

"Thanks, mister. I thought for sure that I was a goner until you and your friend showed up."

"I'm glad we were able to be of assistance," Waverly said.

The woman took another sip from the canteen, holding it shakily with both hands, and then returned it to Waverly, who hung it on his saddle horn.

Chandler rode up, dismounted, and stood beside Waverly. "I don't think they'll be back," he said.

"Thank heaven," the woman said with sincere relief as she removed her hat and ran her hand through her hair. Despite the fact that she had just experienced a harrowing ordeal and was obviously trail weary, there was a stunning physical beauty about her. She appeared to be in her late twenties. Her hair was straw-colored and fell just short of her shoulders. Her eyes were large and dark brown and, in spite of the tears she had just cried, were of a remarkable clarity and brilliance. Her cheekbones were high, and her lips were perfectly formed around a row of even white teeth. "We owe you our lives," she said.

Waverly smiled. "I'm John Waverly. This is Dell Chandler."

"I'm Nora Stuart. This is my brother, Orrin."

Waverly and Chandler touched the brims of their Stetsons and then shook hands with Orrin, who grinned at them broadly. He was about thirty, five-foot-eight, with hair the color of his sister's. There was a good-natured attitude about him that made one feel comfortable.

"What are you doing way out here by yourselves?" Chandler asked.

"I'm a freighter. I operate out of St. Jo," he replied.

Waverly glanced at the wagon, which had several wooden crates in its bed. "Those boys waylay you, did they?"

Orrin nodded. "They jumped us on the road and forced us into this clearing. I think they had it in mind to kill us and take my team and cargo."

"More than likely," Waverly said. Turning his attention to Nora, he added, "This could be dangerous work for a lady."

"Oh, Nora doesn't usually ride with me. I just happened to be passing through Myersville, and she has a friend there."

"I see. Well, it's late and not a good idea to be on the road at this hour. We're camped a short distance from here. We have plenty of food left. Why don't you join us for some dinner. You can bed down nearby and get a fresh start in the morning," Waverly suggested.

Nora glanced at her brother and nodded, obviously eager to accept the invitation.

Orrin smiled his appreciation. "I think we'd both like that just fine, Mr. Waverly."

"I'd certainly feel safer," Nora added.

"All right, then it's settled. We'll lead the way."

Orrin helped his sister onto the freight wagon and

then climbed up beside her. He took up the reins, called out to his horses, and soon had the wagon on the road, where Waverly and Chandler led them back to their campsite.

Connors was on his feet, the Henry held loosely in his hands, when he saw the small but noisy entourage pull into camp. He greeted the new arrivals and helped Nora descend from the wagon.

Waverly made the introductions, and within minutes, Nora and Orrin were sitting before the fire with plates and cups in their hands. The others sat with them and drank coffee. While Nora and Orrin ate, Waverly and Chandler related the events of the past half hour to Connors, who listened intently. Shaking his head, he said, "You just can't trust many folks anymore."

"Oh, Mr. Connors, it was an awful experience," Nora said. "Without the help of your friends, I shudder to think what those men might have done."

"Just try to put it out of your mind, miss. It's over and done with now," Connors replied.

She laid her plate on a rock and then held her cup to her lips with both hands as she stared into the fire.

Sensing his sister's discomfort, Orrin sought to change the subject. Glancing at Dugger, he asked, "Is there anything wrong with your friend?"

"Just feeling poorly," Connors answered.

"Nothing serious, I hope."

"War injury. It bothers him from time to time," Connors replied.

Nora looked at Dugger, who still lay under his blankets in a deep sleep. "But he's just a boy."

"Plenty of boys didn't get to go home after the war, miss," Connors said.

"How serious is his injury?" she asked.

"I'm afraid that it's very serious."

She frowned deeply. "And the rest of you—you were injured as well?"

"We were," Connors said as he averted her stare.

"Oh, I'm so sorry. Please forgive me. I had no right to pry into your personal lives. I never intended to make you feel uneasy."

"That's all right," Waverly replied. "Every man's past is a part of him—with some, more so than with others. Don't think we haven't been stared at. It's just something that we have to learn to live with."

"War is such a hideous thing," she said.

"Yes, it is. It's an unfortunate way of resolving differences, but so far, men haven't been able to find an alternative," Waverly stated.

Nora eyed him closely, impressed by his words.

"Where are you bound for?" Orrin asked.

"We had it in mind to go to California," Waverly replied, "but the way Dugger's been getting along . . . well, we may have to change our plans."

"That's a long way."

"We thought we'd see some of the country. None of us have been west of the Mississippi before."

"Nora and I live just outside of St. Jo. It's a little out of your way, but it would be nice if you could pay us a visit."

Waverly exchanged glances with Connors and Chandler, who nodded their approval.

"Actually, we were headed in that direction—a town called Guthrie," Waverly said.

"I know it well. I used to haul freight there before I lost my contract. It's only a few days out of St. Jo. Nora is a great cook. She'd fix you a meal you'd never forget."

"In that case, I suppose we could drop in on you, but you'd better stock up on groceries. Connors here is a big eater," Waverly said with a smile.

Orrin and Nora laughed as they looked at Connors, who rubbed his stomach.

"How long have you lived in St. Jo?" Chandler inquired.

"About a year and a half. Nora and I came west from Illinois after our folks passed away. I started a small freighting business. Did pretty well for a time too. Now, I can barely keep my head above water."

"Competition is fierce, is it?" Chandler asked.

Orrin frowned. "It's more than fierce. It's downright cutthroat. Things used to be good. There were several of us small freighters. We all got along and did just fine. Then, after the war, a man named Carl Ludlow showed up. He built a mercantile, bought one of the better hotels, and decided to start a freight line. He's managed to underbid the rest of us on nearly every job, and gradually he's run most of us out of business. He has more wagons and more men. It's unlikely that any of the rest of us are going to last out the year."

"I'm sorry to hear that," Waverly said. "What will you do if that happens?"

Orrin shrugged. "I don't know. I can't see going to work for Ludlow as some of the others have done. I don't like him, and I don't trust him. Maybe I'll head further west myself . . . take my chances at prospecting."

"And what about you, Nora?"

She smiled. "Orrin is all the family I have left. I suppose if he chooses to move on, I'll have no choice but to go with him."

Waverly sipped his coffee. "I've known men who

spent years in the gold fields. It isn't a very solid base on which to build."

"One strike is all I need," Orrin replied.

"That's the goal of every prospector—to find that one big strike. Ninety-nine out of a hundred never find anything but hard times," Connors inserted.

"Well, it can't hurt to try it for a while anyway."

"I suppose not—not if you don't have anything else going for you," Connors said.

"Why not start a freight business somewhere else? Surely, there are new towns springing up all over the West. They'll need supplies," Waverly suggested.

Orrin hung his head. "I don't know. Maybe I've just soured on the idea."

"You're too young to grow sour, Orrin. You and your sister have plenty of good years ahead of you," Chandler added.

Orrin listened carefully to Chandler's words and seemed to take them to heart. After a pause, he rose to his feet and said, "Well, I thank you for the dinner. I'm a little tired, and I believe I'll turn in."

They wished him a good night.

"Sis, I'll lay out your bedroll under the wagon."

"Thanks, Orrin," Nora said.

Connors rose and gathered the plates and cups. "I'll tend to the cooking utensils before I turn in, Captain."

Chandler also rose to his feet. "Do you want me to take the first watch?"

Waverly shook his head. "I'm not sleepy. I'll wake you in three hours."

Chandler nodded. "Good night, Nora," he said before turning toward his bedroll.

"Good night, Mr. Chandler."

"Aren't you tired, Nora?" Waverly asked.

"No, I'm still a little uneasy. I don't think I can sleep yet. I'll just sit by the fire with you for a while if you don't mind?"

"Not at all. I welcome your company. Would you like some more coffee?"

"No, thank you."

Waverly picked up some sticks and dropped them onto the fire. He hefted the Henry and rested it on a rock beside him.

"Mr. Connors and Mr. Chandler are good men," Nora observed.

"Yes, they are."

"And you are too," she said, regarding him closely.

Waverly smiled.

"They call you captain."

"That was my rank. Chandler was my lieutenant, and Connors my sergeant. Young Dugger over there was a corporal in our unit."

"It seems as though they belong beside you."

"We were together for a long time. We fought side by side. Relationships that are formed in battle are lasting ones," Waverly explained.

"And now that the war is over, you've decided to stick together."

"It seemed like a good idea. We tend to complement one another. We've all worked hard to overcome our physical impairments. Connors, for instance, was an expert marksman. A Henry rifle was like an extension of his hand. When he lost his eye, his depth perception was gone. He had to retrain himself in order to regain his skills. Chandler was and is an expert horseman, but with one arm, even simple tasks like harnessing a horse or hitching a wagon team became problems that he had to train to overcome."

"And you?"

"I was probably the most fortunate. My leg was permanently damaged. Running is impossible. Walking without pain is often a concern. Like the others, I'm a cripple."

"I hadn't noticed."

Waverly considered Nora. It was nice of her to make such a comment, he thought.

She turned up her collar and pulled her coat more closely about her.

Waverly picked up a blanket and draped it over her shoulders. "It's getting cold," he said.

"Thank you. That's much better," she said with a smile as she edged nearer to him.

Chapter Nine

There was a biting nip in the air on the following morning, and they all huddled around the fire warming their hands. Dugger was up and around again and seemed to be feeling better. He was surprised to discover the two new faces in camp and was quickly apprised of the events of the previous day that led to the meeting with Orrin and Nora. Nora assisted with breakfast and immediately demonstrated the cooking skills that her brother had touted. She brought out a crate of eggs she had in the wagon and whipped up a batch. They were light and airy, and the coffee went down better.

"You've got a job with us any time, Nora," Connors announced as he dropped another spoonful of eggs onto his plate.

"I'm glad you like it," Nora said with a grin.

"I usually do the cooking, Nora. I guess now my life is going to be anything but easy," Waverly announced.

"These are the best eggs I've ever had," Dugger chipped in.

"See what I mean." Turning to Dugger, Waverly said, "Why don't you go back to sleep."

"I've got a feeling that you men can take pretty good care of yourselves. All you need is a woman's touch from time to time," Nora said.

"Sure couldn't hurt," Connors put in. "Especially a pretty one!"

Nora blushed.

They broke camp and readied the horses. Before mounting the freight wagon, Nora approached Waverly and extended her hand. "Thank you again, Mr. Waverly. You and your friends have given my brother and me a second chance."

Taking her hand, Waverly said, "Good luck to you, Nora. I hope that everything works out for you." He took her arm and helped her onto the wagon.

"You boys make sure you get to St. Jo for a visit now," Orrin stated. "We have a small place just south of town. Most everybody knows where we live."

"If all goes well, we should be there in three or four days," Waverly said.

Orrin and Nora waved as they pulled out. The heavy wagon jostled noisily as Orrin directed the horses back to the main road.

"Nice people," Connors said to Waverly.

"Yes, they are."

"You seemed to get along pretty well with Nora."

Waverly looked at Connors askance. "As a matter of fact, we got along just fine."

Connors permitted himself a small grin. "Glad to hear it, Captain," he said as he turned for his horse.

They reached Guthrie on the afternoon of the next day. It was a small community—a population of 212, according to the city limits sign. The main street had the usual assortment of stores and shops—including a mercantile, a hotel, a boarding house, a livery, a dress shop, and a pair of saloons. They made their way directly to the livery, where they saw an old man sitting on a wooden chair next to a corral post. His clothes were dingy, his Stetson battered. A pipe stuck out of the corner of his mouth. Slowly, he rose to his feet as they approached.

"You want to stable your horses for the night, gents?" he asked solicitously.

"That will be fine. How much?" Waverly asked as he and the others dismounted.

The ostler looked them over carefully. "Can you part with three dollars?"

"Sounds reasonable," Waverly replied as he reached into his pocket.

"That's all right. You can pay me when you leave. By the way, my name's McConnell, but you can call me Gramps. Most everybody does."

"Business a little slow, is it?" Waverly asked as he glanced at the nearly empty corral.

"Slow doesn't describe it. You're the first customers I've had this week."

"Your town isn't exactly on the main road west," Connors said.

"Not exactly, son. Things are pretty quiet around here."

They removed their saddlebags and headed for the hotel, a respectable looking structure with a fancy sign above the entry that read THE VINCENT HOUSE.

Turning to Chandler, Waverly asked, "Your wife's family?"

"Her cousin's name. The Vincents own the hotel and

the millinery shop where Marion works now," Chandler explained.

Waverly nodded.

The hotel lobby was a tidy room decorated with stuffed chairs and potted ferns. The clerk was polite, gave them their room keys, and arranged for hot water for baths. An hour and a half later, they were clean and presentable again and in search of a meal. They passed through the lobby again and into the adjoining hotel restaurant, where they paused in front of a chalkboard that advertised the day's offerings.

"I'll part company with you here. I'll have something to eat later," Chandler said as he looked at the others uneasily.

Waverly nodded.

Connors extended his hand. "Good luck, Lieutenant."

"Thanks, Brad," Chandler replied as he shook Connors' hand firmly.

Dugger completed a makeshift salute as he regarded Chandler with sadness in his eyes.

Chandler turned and walked away, leaving the others staring after him as he made his way through the hotel door and into the street. He passed the mercantile and one of the saloons before he spotted a barber shop. He hesitated for a long moment, feeling the coarse growth on his face, and then entered. The barber, a short, mustached man with a clean white shirt, looked at him askance at first, apparently uncomfortable at seeing Chandler's missing limb. He smiled, however, and motioned Chandler into a chair.

"Haircut?"

"No, just a shave."

The barber nodded as he placed the chair cloth over

Chandler and began to whip up some lather. He made small talk, but Chandler's mind was elsewhere and he responded in monosyllables. Five minutes later he climbed out of the chair, paid the barber, and left. His face was now smooth and clean, and he felt a bit less self-conscious as he walked down the boardwalk. He read the signs over the stores in Guthrie as he moved along, searching for one in particular. When he spotted the millinery, he stopped and looked around. There was no one about. He reached into his coat pocket and wrapped his hand around the letter that he had carried for so long now. He started to pull it out and read it again, but he changed his mind, for he knew every word by heart. For a long time, he stood on the boardwalk, uncertain, uncomfortable, but in the end, he took a deep breath and started across the street. He paused to avoid a small boy who was running by, pushing a metal ring with a stick. The youngster distracted him for a moment, but he resumed and entered the millinery.

It was a small shop, pleasantly scented and colorful to the eye. Dozens of hats were prominently displayed. A long counter lay just to the left of the entrance, aligned with ribbons, hatpins, lace, and several bolts of material. Chandler stood uneasily in the shop, glancing about awkwardly at more fancy things than he had ever seen before in one place. In a moment, a young woman emerged from a back room and stood behind the counter. She was unusually pretty, with chestnut colored hair, brown eyes, and a peaches and cream complexion. She wore a white dress with a lace collar. As she placed her hands on the counter and regarded Chandler closely, she struck an almost fragile pose.

"Hello, Dell," she said with the slightest smile.

"Hello, Marion. It's good to see you again."

"I wasn't certain how you'd feel, but I knew that, sooner or later, you'd be coming."

Chandler shifted his feet uneasily.

Marion's eyes focused on Chandler's empty shirt sleeve, which was pinned at the shoulder. "Was it bad—the pain, I mean?"

Chandler nodded. "It was, but it's over now."

"Not really. It will never be over."

Chandler felt his stomach tighten. "There are some things that you have to learn to live with, Marion."

"There are some things you can't live with, Dell. I tried very hard to make that clear to you in my letter."

"You did. I wrote you after I received it, trying to explain how I felt."

"I got your letter. It caught up with me several months later . . . after I moved here."

Chandler moistened his lips with his tongue as he awaited her next words.

"It . . . didn't change anything. I've never been a strong person. You know that. Some women can live with burdens. I've never had that kind of fortitude. To spend my life with a man who . . ."

"Who is a cripple?"

Marion's face tensed. "Don't say it that way."

"That's the way it is."

"I didn't want to hurt you, Dell," she said in a voice that was very nearly pleading.

Chandler, realizing that he had been holding his breath, exhaled deeply. "I know. I suppose I don't have the right to expect anything like this from you. It's more than a wife should be asked to do—to sacrifice a chance for a normal life. I imagine it was just human nature—or male weakness on my part, whatever one calls it—to come here and confront you after you made things so clear in your letter. But you see, I had to be sure of something else as well."

Marion considered him closely. "You mean . . . is there another man?"

Chandler nodded.

"No, Dell. There never was and, frankly, I'm not sure there ever will be. I loved you, and I still love you in my own way. I suppose I always will," she said as she picked up some ribbon and wound it through her fingers. "It's just that I'm not the kind of woman who could endure all the stares and the behind-the-back comments from people every time the two of us went into a restaurant or walked down the street."

Chandler looked down at the floor. "I can't say that I blame you for that. I'm having a difficult time getting used to it myself."

Marion's lips parted as though she wanted to speak but did not know exactly what to say. Finally, she said, "I'm so sorry for you, Dell. When I received the news of your injury, I cried for days. I knew how much pain you must have been in . . . how much you must have suffered. When I finally got over the inner hurt, I decided then and there that I didn't want to cry anymore. I knew that it had to come to an end. Please don't hold it against me. I just knew that I couldn't be happy trying to go through with it. I could pretend to do so, but that would be cruel, and in the end, that would be worse for both of us."

Chandler wanted to engage her in an argument—to attempt to change her mind—for he knew that he still loved her with all his heart. He also knew, however, that such an action would prove futile. Just as in combat, there were times when a tactical withdrawal was the only viable alternative when engaging a superior force.

"I . . . I understand and respect your feelings, Marion. I'll move on. I'll let you know where to reach me when I finally get settled, and if there's ever anything you need, don't hesitate to write me."

"Are you still with your friends—Captain Waverly and Sergeant Connors?"

"Yes, and Dugger."

"The boy? How is he doing?"

"Not well, I'm afraid. His spells are getting worse."

She shook her head in despair. "Such a tragedy. So many fine young men scarred for life. So many did not even walk away."

Chandler nodded.

"Where will you go?"

"West. We had planned on California, but that may change, depending on Dugger's condition. We met some folks from St. Jo, nice folks named Stuart. We got them out of some trouble, and they were very grateful. They invited us to visit them. We'll probably head in that direction, stay over for a few days."

"I see. Take care of yourself, Dell. I hope that you and your friends find what you're looking for."

"Thank you, Marion. I wish you all the best as well."

She extended her hand, and Chandler took it. He looked at her for what he believed would be the last time, and then he turned and left the shop. He walked along the boardwalk back toward the hotel, but he paused when he reached the saloon. A tune from the piano caught his ear, and he hesitated for some time as he listened to the music. He thought it strange that he should be drawn to the melody, for it was not a song that he had ever liked, yet it reminded him of times that had been good. He pushed his way through the batwing doors and found a table off in a corner. The saloon was very nearly empty, and the bartender approached him immediately and asked him his pleasure. Chandler ordered whiskey.

Two hours later, Chandler was sitting in the same spot, lost in the music of the piano player, his drink untouched. A familiar voice broke his train of thought, and he glanced up, failing at first to recognize Waverly, who slid into a chair beside him.

"Are you all right?" Waverly asked.

Chandler nodded.

"Do you want to talk about it?"

"There's nothing to talk about. I had a dwindling hope that we could be together again, but it wasn't meant to be."

Waverly's lips tightened as he pushed back his Stetson. "The injury has been hard on you. Imagine how she must feel."

"I know."

"Maybe . . . in time—"

"No. Marion is a good woman in most every way, but she's not equipped to handle this kind of adversity."

"I see. Nevertheless, we were planning on riding on in the morning. If you want to stay in town for a while—"

"There's no need. I'll be leaving with you."

Waverly nodded. "Did you have anything to eat?"

Chandler shrugged. "I'll get a sandwich later."

Waverly considered Chandler for a long moment. Respecting his friend's need to be left with his thoughts, he rose to his feet. "I'll be at the hotel if you need me."

Chandler remained in the saloon for several more hours. A handful of patrons drifted in and out. The piano player had long since departed, and finally, the bartender announced that he was closing. It was very late when Chandler made his way back to the hotel.

Chapter Ten

Their first sight of St. Jo was an impressive one. It was, undoubtedly, the biggest city they had seen since they had begun their journey west. Hotels, boarding houses, saloons, stores, shops, churches, a railroad depot, people bustling about—it was the most activity they had encountered in some time.

Dugger, more than the others, was awed by what he saw. "How many folks do you figure live here?" he asked.

"I'd say close to ten thousand," Waverly replied.

Dugger let out a low whistle.

"Look there. They even have an opera house," Connors observed, pointing at an ornate structure decorated in bright paint and adorned with a red canopy, beneath which flashy posters advertised performers in eye-catching costumes.

"Who are those people on those flyers?" Dugger asked.

"Those are thespians," Chandler returned.

Dugger shot a questioning look at him.

"Actors and actresses," Waverly added with a smile.

"Oh." Dugger gave a knowing nod, but it was clear that he was at sea.

"The captain and the lieutenant have formal educations, Tim. What they mean to say is that actors are people who dress up in fancy clothes and pretend to be other people. They stand on a stage in front of an audience and use a passel of pretty words in a way that most common folks don't talk."

"Like politicians, you mean?"

The others chuckled.

"Not exactly. Actors relate stories written by famous writers like Shakespeare and Dickens," Waverly explained.

"They get paid for it?"

"They do, and the good ones are paid very well."

"Seems like a waste of money, paying to watch someone pretending to be someone he isn't," Dugger offered.

"It's entertainment," Chandler added, "more refined entertainment than saloon girls or dance hall performers. It can also be educational."

"You've never seen a stage performance before?" Connors asked.

"No, sir, I have not."

"Well, maybe we can sit in on one before we leave town," Waverly suggested.

"That's fine by me," Dugger returned, eyeing one of the posters closely. It depicted a woman with long red hair wearing a form-fitting evening gown. "I've never seen a lady dressed like that before. She sure is beautiful. It might be worth paying to see after all."

Connors grinned. "It might be at that, Tim, my boy."

They got directions from a local about stabling their

horses. He also recommended a boarding house with comfortable beds and good meals. They took his advice and were not disappointed, for they were soon rested and clean shaved and had a tasty lunch in their stomachs. Then, they set out on foot to have a closer look at St. Jo.

Simply standing on the boardwalk and watching people pass by was an experience in itself. There were people of all walks of life, and their trades often left signs on their persons. The blacksmith, for instance, wore his leather apron. His hands and arms were muscular and well developed. The businessmen who trailed in and out of the bank wore spotless suits and derbies more often than Stetsons. A multitude of people of different backgrounds flooded through the streets. There were Orientals, Mexicans, and Indians. Some were just wayfarers; others fulfilled vital roles within the community. There were merchants, cowboys, gamblers, grifters, and saloon girls. An Indian woman carrying a papoose on her back strolled by. A minister nodded and smiled as he walked along the boardwalk.

A long, low whistle caught their ears, and they saw a worm of dark smoke rising in the distance. A train was pulling into the depot, and they made their way to the track bed to watch the excitement as the engine drew to a slow, grudging halt amidst a backdrop of smoke, sparks, and soot. Passengers disembarked onto a long wooden platform as baggage handlers rushed to remove boxes, crates, and barrels from the supply cars. A conductor in a decorative black suit with large silver buttons emerged from the lead passenger car and checked his pocket watch before strutting into the depot with an expression of pride on his face.

Connors stood with his hands in his pockets and

stared at the parade of activity. "You know, I always thought that there was something intriguing about trains. I do believe that I could stand and watch them for hours."

"I believe I could too," Dugger announced.

"The iron horse . . . it will be the next door to the opening of the West," Waverly proclaimed.

"Where does this train come from, Captain?" Dugger inquired.

"All the way from Hannibal. Some day there will be iron rails all the way to the Pacific."

"The ocean?"

"That's right, Tim. We'll see it sooner than you think," Waverly said.

"I've never seen an ocean."

"It's bigger than any prairie, bigger than any mountain range," Waverly explained.

"You've seen one?"

"I've seen the Atlantic."

"I have too," Chandler added.

"Same here," Connors echoed, "but the Pacific is bigger yet, although not that you'd notice the difference."

Dugger shook his head as he considered the concept. "I wonder if I will ever see it," he mused.

The others looked at each other.

"Of course, you will," Connors put in. "We'll all see it together. California borders on the Pacific, you know."

Dugger nodded as he turned away and stared at something off in the distance.

A few minutes later they left the depot and headed toward the main street of the city. A newspaper office caught Waverly's eye, and he paused and stared through the window, watching a typesetter plying his skills. The front page of the next edition was posted on the window. It featured a banner and article about the Radical Union Party, which Waverly read while the others stood beside him. Finally, he entered the office and purchased a copy, which he folded and placed in his coat pocket.

"You sure do read a lot of newspapers, Captain," Dugger noted.

"It's important for a man to keep abreast of the latest news. It makes him a better citizen. It also keeps him informed of his country's progress—the direction it's taking. You should get in the habit of reading the news on a regular basis, Tim."

"I guess that makes sense, Captain," Dugger replied.

They continued down the street, observing the heavy volume of horse, wagon, and foot traffic and taking in the wide variety of notions offered in the many stores. One mercantile had a display on the Pony Express in its window. A saddle was mounted on a wooden stand. Upon it was a leather mochila. In front of the display was a sign alleging that the equipment was actually used by riders for the Pony Express. A parchment documented the brief history of the organization and its noteworthy accomplishments.

"I always had a hankering to ride for the Pony Express," Dugger announced.

"You might've succeeded—you're light and you sit a saddle well enough, but you're too late. The Pony Express didn't even last a year," Connors explained.

"What happened to it?"

"It became obsolete," Chandler said. "The telegraph put it out of business. Messages can be sent over copper wire in a matter of minutes today."

"There's still a need for mail though."

"Yes, but stages and trains can do the job well enough," Chandler replied.

Dugger shook his head ruefully. "That's sure a shame."

"It's called progress," Waverly put in. "It's what you can read about in newspapers, just as I was telling you. Sometimes good things fall by the wayside when speed or quality or money are involved. I don't imagine that the horse will be the principal mode of transportation in the West some day."

"Well, what will, Captain?" Dugger asked, amazed at such a concept.

Waverly shrugged. "Probably some mechanical device that has an engine in it—like a locomotive."

Dugger shrugged.

"Cheer up, Tim. It won't be for many years to come. You'll probably be an old-timer sitting in a rocking chair by then."

They all smiled.

They continued along the boardwalk for several blocks when they spotted a long low building with a sign jutting from the roof that read STUART'S FREIGHT. Connors and Dugger led the way inside, and Chandler and Waverly followed. They immediately saw Nora sitting on a stool behind the counter. She glanced up from a document she was reading, and when she saw them, she beamed broadly.

"Why, gentlemen, it's certainly a pleasure to see you again," she said as she rounded the counter, patted Dugger on the shoulder, and then proceeded to shake hands with the others. She wore a white blouse with frills across the bodice. A small silver pin in the shape of a swan hung just beneath her collar. Her skirt was charcoal gray with black buttons running down the side. Her hair was neatly swept up just above her shoulders. Her face looked fresh and clean, and she offered an even more striking appearance than the one she had presented on the trail when they had first seen her.

"It's sure good to see you again, Nora," Dugger announced.

"Well, the feeling is mutual, Tim. When did you men get into town?"

"Just a few hours ago," Connors answered.

"In that case, how about joining Orrin and me for dinner tonight at our place?"

"Sounds good," Chandler replied.

"I can smell chicken and dumplings already," Connors chimed in.

"Then, chicken and dumplings it shall be," Nora returned.

"Where's Orrin?" Waverly asked.

"Oh, he's at the blacksmith's, having a wheel looked at. He'll be delighted when I tell him that you're here. Now, just take the south road out of town for about a mile and a half. It will lead you directly to our place. You can't miss it. I'd consider taking you out there right now, but somebody's got to watch the office—even though we haven't had any business to speak of since we got back."

"Pretty slow, huh?" Connors asked.

"Like a graveyard. Another month or two of this and we might just as well take down the sign."

"You'd think that in a community of this size there would be more than enough business to go around," Waverly said.

"There is"—Nora said, pausing—"but the small outfits like us just keep getting underbid by Carl Ludlow's operation. Oh, I can't blame the customers. They're looking for a bargain, and Ludlow gives them the best deal."

"How can he continue to do that?" Chandler inquired.

"He's willing to sacrifice a few dollars in order to corner the market. In the long run, he'll win all the marbles anyway. It's only a matter of time."

"I'd be willing to spend a few dollars extra just to do business with a pretty gal like you," Connors said.

Nora laughed out loud. "Why, thank you, sir. You've just made my day."

Waverly glanced around the office. It was small but remarkably tidy. A pair of windows sparkled, admitting light across a hardwood floor. The counter had several neat stacks of paper on it. A back room offered a glimpse of a safe off in one corner. "You certainly have the cleanest office I've ever seen."

"When you don't have much business, you have plenty of time to keep things clean, Captain," she said.

"Well, I'm sorry that things haven't picked up for you. Maybe you should consider seeking another line of work. It's hard to buck a big operation," Waverly said.

"Oh, let's not discuss that now. I don't want to burden you with our problems. I want us all to be happy tonight. We'll have dinner, and you can tell Orrin and me about your travels."

"We'll be there."

"Six o'clock suit you?"

"Six o'clock it is," Waverly said, tipping the brim of his Stetson. He nodded to the others, and they left the office.

As they continued along the boardwalk, they discussed the Stuarts.

"Nice gal," Connors said. "I hate to see good folks like her and Orrin down in the mouth."

"Yeah, it sure doesn't seem fair," Dugger added.

"That's one of the drawbacks of progress. The little man often falls by the wayside," Waverly said.

"I thought progress was important," Dugger returned.

"It is, but sometimes society has a hard time adjusting to changes. We have to do a better job of learning how to cope with it—to roll with the punches, so to speak—or we get left behind or buried over."

They passed onto another street, where they were momentarily stunned by what they saw. A stately hotel loomed before them. Its facade, composed of massive squares of stone, gave it a grandiloquent appearance. A long porch, supported by ornately carved pillars, extended across the entire length of the front of the building. Handrails painted in white added an inviting flavor to its overall appearance. Over a pair of highly burnished doors that marked the entrance, a sign read HOTEL DELUXE, CARL LUDLOW . . . OWNER AND PROPRIETOR.

"Whoa, that sure is fancy!" Connors exclaimed.

"I'll say," Dugger chimed in.

Further down the street was a mercantile bearing the same name, and on the next block was Ludlow's freight office.

"Looks like this Carl Ludlow has done all right for himself," Chandler observed.

They spent the rest of the afternoon familiarizing themselves with St. Jo before they returned to the boarding house and cleaned up for dinner. Following Nora's directions, they soon found themselves in front of a small ranch house with a white picket fence. The residence was modest in design and appearance, but it looked like a comfortable place for a man to hang his hat or stretch out in a chair on the front porch.

They dismounted and tied their horses to a hitching rail. Before they even stepped up onto the porch, Orrin came through the door and grinned at them as he wrung their hands warmly. He ushered them into the house, where they were invited to hang their Stetsons on a hat tree. The room was warm and cheerful. A huge china cabinet adorned one wall. Comfortable looking arm-chairs were positioned around a stone fireplace. Colorful rugs were scattered across a hardwood floor, and a pretty paper with a floral pattern dressed the walls.

A moment later Nora entered and flashed her friend-ly smile. She wore a light green, floor-length dress with small white buttons. A matching green ribbon ran through her hair, offering a pleasant contrast to her dark eyes.

"Thank you for joining us for dinner, gentlemen. You're right on time. Please come this way. The table is set."

They followed her into an adjoining room, where a long table lay before them, decorated with shiny plates, cups and saucers, and cloth napkins.

"Sit wherever you're comfortable. I'll have the food out in a moment," she announced before disappearing into the kitchen. A minute later she emerged carrying a sizable platter with a mountain of fried chicken on it. On her second trip, she toted in mashed potatoes and gravy. Next, she placed cornbread and greens before them. As they began the meal, she hustled solicitously about the table with a coffeepot, filling their cups as they dug into the tasty meal.

"I declare, Nora, I could smell the aroma from this

chicken all the way from St. Jo," Connors announced between huge bites of meat.

"Best dumplings I ever had, Nora," Dugger said.

"I've found that men generally have short memories as far as their stomachs are concerned. You'll likely forget this meal within a week or two," Nora came back.

"No, ma'am, not me," Dugger said as he placed a spoonful of potatoes in his mouth.

She smiled. "I'm glad you like it, Tim." She sat down after a time and ate a few bites before she asked if anyone desired anything else.

"We're fine, Nora," Waverly answered. "Please enjoy the meal with us."

"Thank you, Captain, I shall."

In time, the conversation turned away from the meal.

"We strolled around town today and saw several businesses owned by your competitor," Chandler said before taking a sip of coffee.

Orrin frowned. "Yeah, he's done pretty well for himself."

"He's not thinking about running for mayor, is he?" Connors asked with a wink. "I sure can't tolerate politicians."

"Not hardly," Orrin said. "He seems to be a man who's mainly concerned with running his businesses."

"Does he live in town?" Chandler asked.

"He keeps a room at his hotel. He uses it when he's in St. Jo. Otherwise, he's got a small spread a few miles out of town. No cattle. A few small crops. A nice home, so they tell me. I think he just likes to keep out of the public eye."

"Yes, but his name certainly appears in the public domain," Nora added.

Waverly folded his napkin and dropped it beside his

plate. "When we first met on the trail, you said that you didn't trust him, Orrin. Why is that?"

Orrin shrugged. "Nothing I can put my finger on—just rumors and hearsay."

"Where's he from?"

"They say he's from Mississippi. The story is that he had a small plantation that was destroyed during the war. He sold his land and whatever else he could salvage and moved west to get a clean start."

"Sounds like a lot of men," Chandler said with a knowing look.

Waverly nodded.

"Well, if you want to stay in the freight business around here, maybe you won't have any choice but to throw in with Ludlow," Connors suggested.

"I couldn't do that. You see, I don't like some of the men who work for him. They're the rough crowd in St. Jo. Not that I can't handle myself, but when I was younger, I got into some small scrapes back in Illinois. I promised my mother when she was on her sick bed that I'd straighten out. I did, and I don't have any intention of falling back into that kind of life again."

"And he means it," Nora added. "Our mother would be proud of the way Orrin has conducted himself since she's been gone. He's certainly done a fine job of looking after his sister."

Orrin smiled as Nora took his hand.

"Well, whatever happens, I hope that everything works out for both of you," Waverly offered.

"Here, here!" Chandler added.

"Thank you, gentlemen," Nora said as she looked at them fondly. "Now, how about some fresh blueberry pie?"

They all declined except for Connors, who nodded eagerly.

The others sipped their coffee as they watched Nora place a plate containing a quarter of a blueberry pie in front of Connors, who immediately attacked it with his fork.

"I swear," Chandler said, "I don't know where you put it."

Connors just winked as he continued to eat.

"You know, Nora, we discovered that there's an opera house here in St. Jo. We thought about attending the evening performance tomorrow. How would you and Orrin like to come as our guests?" Waverly asked.

Nora's eyes widened as she glanced at Orrin. "Why, we'd love to, Captain!"

"Good. Why don't we take you to dinner before the performance. We can meet at the restaurant of your choice."

"O'Brien's is my favorite. It's just a few blocks from the theater," Nora suggested.

"O'Brien's it is then. Shall we meet there at . . . six?"

"That would be wonderful."

"In the meantime, before it gets dark, I'd like to show you around the place. There's a nice stream out back that has good trout," Orrin said.

"I'd like to see it," Chandler said, pushing himself away from the table.

"Me too," Dugger added.

"I'll join you as soon as I finish my dessert," Connors put in.

Waverly rose from the table. "I think I'll just sit on the porch for a while and let my meal digest."

"And I'll join you, Captain," Nora said.

Orrin led the others around the back of the house while Waverly and Nora sat on some chairs near the front door. It was a pleasant Missouri evening with scudding clouds high in the sky that were quickly fading in the distance. A songbird trilled from somewhere off in a thicket, and a fresh, clean smell hung in the air.

"You're the nicest people we've had the pleasure to meet in some time, Captain," Nora ventured.

"Thank you, Nora. That's kind of you to say. Please call me John."

She smiled.

"You and Orrin have a fine place here."

"We both like it, but there's still a mortgage on the property, and it's harder and harder to get it together every month. I'm afraid we'll have to sell it back to the bank," she said sadly.

"There are other places, other lines of work. We all have to keep looking until we find the direction that's right for us."

She considered him closely. "What is it exactly that you're looking for, John?"

Waverly stared off into the distance. "Maybe just a quiet valley where there is no violence . . . a place where homes and ranches and farms can be built instead of destroyed. There are enough scars on this country now."

After a long pause, Nora said, "Is such a thing truly possible?"

Waverly looked at her closely. "I don't know. Everywhere you go, one man seems to be trying to pick another man's pocket."

"Do you think that you can avoid all of that by moving west?"

"No, not really. People are people—wherever you

go." He shook his head. "I don't know. Maybe I'm just running away."

"You and the others don't look like the kind of men who would run from anything."

"We never have yet, but a man gets tired, disappointed, disillusioned. Sometimes, when he's seriously hurt, he loses his edge. You know, after the war, I read a newspaper editorial. In it, the author referred to men like us as ghosts—ghosts from the past, men whom the public would like to forget . . . maybe because we remind them of the ugliness of war and what went wrong in our country. I suppose, in some regards, he was right, though. We are ghosts—ghosts of what we once were."

"I think I can understand that, John. I hope that you never get hurt again in any way."

Waverly regarded her closely. He thought that she looked exceptionally beautiful as she sat beside him, talking to him as no one else had for some time. He believed that she understood and respected his feelings. He concluded that he liked her. He liked her very much.

Chapter Eleven

O'Brien's was a friendly Irish eatery that special-
ized in meat, potatoes, and cabbage. A variety of stews
were available with beef and lamb as the principal
ingredients. Beer, strong coffee, and tea were offered as
the house beverages. O'Brien was a big beefy Irishman
who welcomed all his guests personally. His waiters
looked alike in appearance—hefty, mustached, with
large white cloths that served as aprons around their
waists.

Orrin and Nora ordered their favorite—lamb stew—
as did Waverly and Connors. Chandler and Dugger
opted for boiled beef, potatoes, and cabbage. It was a
hearty meal, and they all exchanged favorable comments about the portions as well as the quality.

They left the restaurant in a convivial mood and
strolled down the boardwalk to the opera house. They
paid their admission and were ushered into a large
room that was both comfortable and appealing, with
soft cushioned seats tiered down to a long stage that
was illuminated by gaslight. The painted stage scenery

depicted the interior of a country home, and the set contained an attractive arrangement of furniture, rugs, and a false fireplace. At the appointed time, a well dressed man in a coat and tails stepped onto the stage and welcomed the audience. He introduced the play, a comedy titled *A Visit from Uncle Thaddeus,* listed some of the credits of the lead performers, and then disappeared into the wings. Soon, the principal actor and actress appeared and began to move about the stage, reciting their lines with great emotion. They were attractive people, dressed in the latest fashions, and they performed with that rare panache that marked the professional thespian. The plot of the play concerned a conniving family that had squandered their wealth and were now wooing their rich uncle for additional financial support. The uncle, a miser, cleverly outwitted them at every turn. It was a humorous, witty play, skillfully presented by each and every actor, and the audience responded accordingly with laughter and enthusiasm. At the conclusion, the performers stepped to the front of the stage to take their bows as the audience gave them a rousing ovation.

Nora, who had sat between Waverly and Chandler throughout the performance, seemed particularly delighted with the entire evening. She had whispered several comments to each of them about the various aspects of the play and was enamored of the lovely gowns worn by the actresses.

Dugger was in awe of the pageantry of the theater. He could not find the words to express his amazement.

The six of them could not talk enough about the event, and they carried their conversation from the opera house to the boardwalk, where they stood, as did so many others, and discussed the play for some time.

Finally, Orrin suggested, "There's an ice cream parlor two streets over. How about if we each get a bowl?"

"Oh, Orrin, I baked a cake this afternoon, and I was hoping that everyone could return to the house for some dessert and coffee," Nora said.

"I've heard of ice cream, but I've never had any," Dugger announced.

"I think I'd be better suited with a slice of cake," Connors said.

"Same here," Chandler added.

Waverly turned to Orrin. "Why don't you and Tim get some ice cream while the rest of us return to your house. You can ride back on my mount, and I can share the buggy with Nora."

"Sounds good," Orrin said. "We'll see you shortly."

As Orrin and Dugger crossed the street, the others made their way to the stable, where Chandler and Connors picked up their horses and Waverly and Nora climbed into the buggy. Waverly also left word with the ostler that Orrin would be borrowing his horse for the evening.

An hour later, Nora was refilling everyone's cup while Connors was starting on his third piece of cake.

"Tim doesn't know what he's missing," Connors extolled. "I haven't had a sweet like this since I don't know when . . . it's so light and fluffy."

"I've never seen a man eat like you, Sergeant," Nora claimed.

"Neither have we," Chandler added.

"Any woman who's handy with a skillet and a bowl of batter deserves to have her efforts appreciated," Connors stated.

"How is it that you never seem to put on a pound?" Chandler asked.

"Hard work just keeps it off."

The others chuckled.

A sudden crash of thunder rumbled in the distance, followed by the heavy drone of raindrops on the roof.

Nora stepped to the window and parted the curtain. "It's really coming down. It looks like the boys are going to get wet tonight."

"The sky didn't look like rain today," Connors observed.

"Oh, we have quite a few of these sudden downpours at this time of year."

About ten minutes later, they heard hoofbeats approaching. Nora smiled. "Sounds like the boys finally got here."

"Only one horse," Chandler returned.

A moment later, Orrin walked through the door, his clothes drenched from the rain. He removed his Stetson and stood before them, a troubled look on his face.

"Where's Dugger?" Waverly inquired.

"I don't know exactly," Orrin replied.

"Why, what do you mean?" Nora asked. "Did something happen to him?"

"No, nothing as far as I know."

The others stared at him, awaiting an explanation.

Orrin frowned. "The two of us were walking down the street, heading toward the ice cream parlor, when Tim suddenly stopped. I turned and found him—almost frozen in position, staring at something off in the distance. I did my best to follow his gaze, but I couldn't tell exactly what it was that had captured his attention. The streets were crowded, but I didn't notice anyone in particular, much less anything unusual.

"I walked back toward Tim and asked him what was the matter. He didn't answer. It was as though he was in another world. He muttered something under his breath that I'm not sure I understood, and then suddenly he walked away. I called after him, but it was as though he didn't hear me. When I tried to follow him, I was cut off by a wagon. By the time I reached the corner where I last saw him, he was gone.

"I stood there on the boardwalk for some time, searching the crowd, waiting for Tim to return. He never did. I walked up and down the street for several blocks in each direction, but I couldn't find him."

The others stared at Orrin for a long moment as they digested his story.

Finally, Waverly asked, "What was it that you think Tim said?"

Orrin shrugged. "I'm not sure, but it sounded like he said something about . . . tracks."

Waverly contemplated Orrin's response for some time before he slowly climbed to his feet. "Could he have said . . . Traxler?"

Connors and Chandler stood up in unison and stared at each other.

Orrin considered the name. "He might have. I can't be certain."

Waverly turned toward Connors and Chandler. For some time, their eyes locked.

"We'd best get back to town right away," Waverly said.

"What is it, John? Who is Traxler?" Nora asked, recognizing the effect the name had on them.

"It's a name from the past, Nora . . . the name of a man we knew in the war," Waverly answered somberly, the tone of his voice telling her that he was somewhere far away from her and the parlor in which they stood.

"You don't think that Tim actually saw him, do you?" Connors asked. "I mean . . . is it possible?"

"I don't know," Waverly replied. He reached under his coat, but his hand came up empty. "Orrin, we've left our guns back at the boarding house. Do you have any?"

"I've got an old Navy Colt."

Waverly nodded.

Orrin disappeared into the next room and returned quickly, handing the Colt to Waverly.

Waverly opened the chamber, checked the rounds, and then shut it with a click. He tucked it under his belt and nodded to the others, who wasted no time in heading for the door.

Nora clutched Waverly's arm. "We're coming, too, John. We can help you search for Tim."

"Of course we can," Orrin added, "but we can't leave now—none of us can. The rain's coming down too hard."

"That won't stop us," Connors returned.

"You don't understand. These cloudbursts don't last long, but they're heavy, and they have to be taken seriously. They cause flash flooding. It isn't safe to cross that ravine between here and town when the rain falls this hard. In fact, it's next to impossible. A horse could lose its footing and get hurt. A rider can easily be injured. Believe me, it's happened many a time."

"He's right," Nora added. "Just last month one of our neighbors nearly drowned when he got caught in one of these downpours."

"How long before the road is passable?" Connors asked.

"An hour—not much more than that."

"Surely an hour can't make that much difference to you," Nora said.

"Maybe not, but it might to Dugger," Chandler put in.

"None of you will do Dugger any good if you get hurt yourselves," Orrin returned.

Scowling heavily, Waverly regarded Chandler and Connors. "All right. We'll wait an hour but no more. After that, flood or not, we'll have to take our chances."

They sat down again and stared uneasily at various objects in the room, speaking little, each lost deep within his thoughts. Orrin put another log on the fire and then brushed off his hands. A few minutes later Waverly climbed to his feet and glanced out the window. He pushed his hands into his pockets and stared at the clock on the wall.

Finally, Nora asked, "John . . . who exactly is this Traxler?"

Waverly took a deep breath, exchanged a glance with Chandler and Connors, and then sat down next to them. He leaned forward and rested his hands on his knees. "We encountered him during the war, Nora. He was a Confederate lieutenant."

"Was he the one responsible for your injuries?" Nora asked.

"He was."

"But that was war. Surely, you can't blame an enemy soldier for injuries you sustained in battle."

"Our injuries weren't sustained in battle."

Nora looked puzzled, as did Orrin.

Waverly considered them closely. He started to speak, but his reluctance was apparent, for he obviously felt the subject difficult to broach. "It was late in the war. We were operating behind enemy lines. Our unit was given the assignment of rendezvousing with a courier and escorting him to a designated location. We made contact and were well into our mission when we were ambushed by Rebel forces and forced to take cover in a grove of cottonwoods. We held our own for some time, but we were heavily outnumbered and out-gunned, and our small force was slowly but surely being cut to pieces. The courier took a round in the chest. I knew at once that the wound was a fatal one. Before he died, however, he told us what it was that he was carrying in his saddlebags—fifty thousand dollars in currency that was to be used to finance a Secret Service operation. Although we were unable to deliver the money, we did the next best thing—we made certain it did not fall into Confederate hands. We buried the saddlebags not far from the body of the courier. There were only five of us who knew the contents of those saddlebags. Besides Lieutenant Chandler, Sergeant Connors, Corporal Dugger, and me, one other soldier, Sergeant Draper, was present when the courier revealed his mission and the contents of the saddlebags he had been dispatched to transport.

"We fought on, until we were out of ammunition and completely surrounded. At that point, there were eight of us left. It was then that I gave the order to surrender. We were quickly taken prisoners, disarmed, and searched before we were ordered to travel on foot to the Rebels' nearest outpost. There, we were placed in a temporary holding area, under heavy guard. We were interrogated briefly by a Confederate captain who, I can assure you, obtained no information whatsoever from any of us. We remained there for only a day and a half before we were transported by wagon for some distance to what could best be described as a makeshift prisoner of war camp. A stockade-like arrangement with a heavy complement of guards became our home for the next three weeks. While there, we ate one meal a day of watered down soup, some coffee, and maggot-infested bread. Occasionally, we were given a plate of collard greens. We were offered little water, with almost none for washing. But the dietary and sanitary conditions themselves were nothing compared to the physical abuse we endured. Daily beatings were common. With the beatings, the lack of proper nutrition, and the inactivity, we grew weaker with each passing day.

"The principal tormentor in camp was a lieutenant named Traxler. More animal than man, he derived pleasure from inflicting pain. He looked upon us not as prisoners of war or as human beings, but as some kind of living specimens that he could taunt and humiliate in every conceivable way. His only goal seemed to be the eventual destruction of each and every one of us through the most pain-filled and lingering methods possible.

"There were some half a dozen men in the stockade when we first arrived, all in the final stages of existence, clutching tenaciously to life, but losing their battles one at a time. They went first. We carried out their bodies one by one and were forced to bury them unceremoniously in unmarked plots of ground. Then, Traxler turned his full attention to the men in our unit. As the ranking officer, I had made numerous efforts to invoke the rules of conduct for an officer and a gentleman in regard to the humane treatment of prisoners of war. My words had always fallen on deaf ears, for he merely sneered at me as if he were the only law and no one would deprive him of his pleasure in the way he dealt with the prisoners in his charge. A few of the guards in his command seemed to delight in witnessing the torture he inflicted, but most of them were repulsed by him. They feared him, however, and went along with his brutality out of sheer will to stay out of his disfavor.

"One by one, the men in our unit began to fail. We contemplated, even planned a breakout, but we knew that such an action was impossible. In our physical state, unarmed, unequipped, and heavily outnumbered, we knew that such a consideration was doomed to total failure and would probably result in worse treatment or even sudden death. Even so, we concluded that dying in an attempt to regain our freedom would have been preferable to being tortured at Traxler's hand.

"One day, we awoke to find that there were only five of us left—Chandler, Connors, Dugger, Draper, and I. The last three days had marked the passing of two young privates in my command. It was at that point that we determined to make an attempt to escape. That day we devised a plan. In retrospect, I think we all believed that it had no chance of succeeding, but we were at our wits' end, and we wanted to die with some dignity—as soldiers. Before we even put our plan into action, however, something unprecedented occurred. We were taken into the middle of the compound, where we were told that we were being transferred to another camp. We could only interpret such news as a renewed hope of salvation. Traxler and two armed guards herded us outside the stockade. They were mounted and had an extra horse in tow. We were on foot. We were so weak we could hardly walk. We stumbled along, but the possibility of being transferred to the command of another gave us some small spark of energy, and we trudged on.

"We had gone no more than two miles, however, when we were ordered to halt. Traxler then directed his guards to stake us out on the ground. We realized at that moment that the story of a transfer was a fabrication, that Traxler's intent was to torture and kill us. For what reason he chose to end our lives miles away from the stockade, in this fashion, we didn't know. Strangely enough, however, he didn't have Sergeant Draper tied down. Instead, he ordered the guards to lead Draper away. At the time, we didn't understand Traxler's actions, but it didn't take us long to draw the conclusion that Draper must have bought his life by promising Traxler that he would reveal the location of the fifty thousand dollars we had secreted.

"Traxler then went to his saddlebags and removed his favorite weapon he used in torturing his prisoners—a short, stout cudgel. For the next thirty minutes, he beat us unmercifully. Dugger, he beat about the ribs and the head. The ribs knitted in time, but the injury to his head has resulted in seizures and spells and may prove to cut his life short. With Chandler, it was his ribs and his arm. His arm was so badly mangled that it had to be amputated. Connors sustained injuries to his ribs and head. His eye socket was shattered, and the end result was the loss of his eye. I was the lucky one—three broken ribs and a leg that was so mutilated I nearly lost it. As it is, I'll spend the rest of my life dragging it behind me."

For some time, there was a long silence as Nora and Orrin digested Waverly's story. They looked at Chandler and Connors with sadness, and Nora's eyes began to moisten as she placed her hand on Waverly's arm.

"I'm so sorry for you . . . for all of you," she said.

Orrin nodded, his face deeply furrowed.

"When we came to—a day . . . two days later, who could tell—we found ourselves in a field hospital. It turned out that we had been discovered by some Union soldiers who were on a reconnaissance mission. We remained there for some time. It was while we were there that we learned that the war had ended. The South had surrendered. We were subsequently transferred to a Union hospital in Nashville. In Chandler's case and in mine, infection had complicated our recoveries. We remained there for months. Following our convalescence, we were discharged. The four of us have remained together ever since. We decided to move west."

"And what became of Traxler?" Orrin asked.

"When we had been returned to Union hands again, we gave a full report of our experiences to the military authorities. An investigation was conducted. The stockade where we had been held was abandoned. There was no record of any troops. We gave a detailed description where we had buried the fifty thousand dollars. Investigators found no money, only the bodies of Sergeant Draper and two Confederate soldiers, along with the decomposed remains of all the others who had died there during the skirmish."

"Then Traxler doublecrossed your Sergeant Draper and his fellow soldiers," Orrin said.

"That's the way it looked. We all thought ill of Draper for a long time, but as the months passed, our hatred for him waned. He had been a good and loyal soldier. He had endured imprisonment and torture at the hands of the enemy. Perhaps, in some ways, he had endured more. Death seemed inevitable. He saw a chance to save his life, and he took it. Many men would have done the same—only sooner. He proved his mettle by fighting the odds and Traxler until he actually believed there was no other way to survive. For him, it had been the eleventh hour and, indeed, it was."

After a pause, Nora asked, "Do you really believe that Tim saw Traxler here in St. Jo?"

Waverly shrugged. "I believe that it's important for us to find Tim as soon as possible."

Chapter Twelve

What had been a hard driving, relentless rain had transformed itself into a soft drizzle. The night sky was beginning to clear, and the moon was stepping out from behind a dark curtain of clouds. The air was fresh and clean and, except for a slight mist, seemed to offer a renewed hope for another day.

The horses made slow progress on the water-soaked road, but as Orrin had indicated, the ravine between the Stuart home and town was now passable with but a few inches of swiftly moving water. Nora had agreed to remain at home in the event that Dugger should per chance return. Orrin, on the other hand, had insisted on accompanying Waverly, Chandler, and Connors back to St. Jo. Orrin and Waverly headed directly for the last place Orrin had seen Dugger. Chandler and Connors returned to the boarding house to secure their guns. From there, they separated, each canvassing a different section of town. For two hours, the four of them walked the rain-slicked boardwalks, checking alleyways and side streets, entering any buildings that were still open in their search for Dugger. Using the opera house as a rendezvous, they reunited at an appointed time. No one had found any trace of Dugger.

"If he left town, he didn't take his horse. I checked the stable. It's still in its stall," Chandler announced.

"I checked with the doctors," Orrin said. "No one has treated anyone matching Dugger's description."

Waverly's brow was heavily furrowed. "We'd best notify the law. We may need more men to search for him."

The others agreed, and they followed Orrin down the boardwalk toward the sheriff's office.

A five-minute walk brought them to a long one-story structure whose entrance was illuminated by a pair of lamps. Orrin was half a dozen paces from the door when a shadowy figure stepped out of an alley and blocked his path on the boardwalk. Orrin halted, as did the others behind him. The figure was that of a big man, about six-foot-two, with sloping shoulders. He wore dark clothing and a black Stetson. A .44 was holstered low on his hip in a style that signalled that he was accustomed to using it. A cigarette stub dangled from the side of his mouth, and a thin wisp of smoke curled up past his face. Three days of stubble gave him a trail-hardened appearance. "You boys wouldn't be lookin' for a friend of yours by any chance?" he asked.

"We would," Orrin replied.

For a long moment, the man did not say anything as he considered them with eyes that were hardly more than slits cut into his face. Finally, he removed his cigarette and said, "You'll find him back at your place."

"Is he all right?" Chandler asked anxiously.

The man sneered, revealing a row of tobacco-stained teeth. "You might say he had a little accident." He dropped the cigarette onto the boardwalk and stepped on it, crushing it under the toe of his boot. He then turned and disappeared down the alley from where he had come.

"Who was that?" Chandler asked.

"His name's Lynch. He's a freighter," Orrin replied.

"He looks like he crawled out from under a rock," Connors added.

"He's a bad one."

They all stared down the black mouth of the alley for a moment. Then, Waverly turned and said, "Let's ride."

The front door to Orrin and Nora's house was wide open, allowing a broad beam of light to flood the porch. As they dismounted, they saw a figure slumped over in a chair near the front steps.

"It looks like Dugger!" Connors called out as he stepped onto the porch and made his way toward the youngster. "Dugger, where have you been? What happened?"

Dugger did not reply.

"Are you all right, boy?" Connors asked as he laid his hand on Dugger's shoulder.

No sooner had Connors touched him than Dugger pitched forward onto the porch.

The others stared on in stunned silence as Connors knelt down beside the lifeless form. Turning Dugger over as gently as possible, Connors winced at the sight of him. "He's . . . he's dead," Connors stammered. "His clothes have been ripped to shreds . . . his skin has been torn from his hands and arms . . . and his face is all but gone."

Chandler knelt down beside Dugger's body. "There are rope burns around his wrists. It looks as though he's been dragged behind a horse."

Waverly's fists clenched as he stared in disbelief at what remained of Corporal Tim Dugger.

For half a minute, no one could speak. Then Orrin looked up, an expression of terror etched on his face. "Nora! Where's Nora?" he shouted.

The thought of Nora seemed to act on the others like an electric charge, bringing them out of their numbed state. Orrin leaped onto the porch and bolted through the front door while Waverly, Chandler, and Connors followed close on his heels, their guns drawn. A quick search of the house proved that Nora was gone, but Waverly found a piece of paper on the parlor table that explained her disappearance. Scribbled in pencil was the message:

IF YOU WANT TO SEE YOUR SISTER AGAIN, BE AT WET ROCK STATION AT NOON TOMORROW. NOTIFY THE LAW AND SHE'LL DIE.

"Nora! They've got Nora! Why would anyone want to hurt Nora?" Orrin gasped as he clutched the note in his hands.

"They don't want Nora, Orrin. They want us," Waverly explained.

"What . . . what do you mean?"

"I mean that Nora's the bait to lure us to this location."

"You mean this man Traxler is behind this?"

Waverly nodded. "It looks that way."

"But . . . I don't—"

"I found it hard to believe at first that Dugger saw him again . . . here in St. Jo . . . after all this time. I thought that Dugger might have just made a mistake or had gotten confused. Now . . . after this has happened . . . well, I believe that Dugger did, by chance, see him and either followed him or confronted him."

"But what made Traxler involve Nora?"

"It's possible that Traxler chanced to see you with Dugger. He may have even seen some of us when we were with you and Nora in town—at the restaurant, the opera house, on the street—anywhere. Either he knows who you are, or he found out. Judging from the way events unfolded so quickly, it's likely that he knows the two of you."

Orrin pondered Waverly's words.

"He realizes that you'll go after your sister, and he also assumes that we'll try to help you."

"And he assumes correctly," Chandler added.

Orrin slumped into a chair. "This is unbelievable! Do you mean to say that this Traxler may be living right here in St. Jo?"

Waverly nodded. "More than likely under a different name. Now, he knows or, at least, suspects that we're alive and may be here in St. Jo as well. He realizes that he's in jeopardy. Even though the war is over, even though it's his word against ours over what took place in that prison camp, the chances of his being convicted for what he has done are very high. He has no choice now but to silence us. As long as we're alive, he's a marked man. By mere chance, we've stumbled upon him. I'm glad of it, but I regret that Nora has ended up in the middle."

"Shouldn't we go to the law?" Orrin asked.

Chandler placed his hand on Orrin's shoulder. "That's your choice, Orrin. It's your sister's life that's on the line, but the note said not to involve the law, and you can lay odds that Lynch or another man is in town right now with his eye on the sheriff's office."

Orrin ran his hand across his mouth. "What can we do?"

"We'll stand with you. We'll do everything we can to get Nora back," Chandler vowed.

Orrin considered the situation for a long time before he slowly, grudgingly nodded.

In the next ten minutes, they wrapped Dugger's body in a blanket and carried him into the house. Connors made a pot of coffee, and the four of them sat around the table to discuss matters.

"First of all, what is this Wet Rock Station?" Waverly asked.

"It's an old relay station used by the Pony Express. It's abandoned now, run down," Orrin explained.

"How far away?"

"It's a good fifteen miles west of here. Nobody goes by there anymore. It's isolated."

"Sounds like a perfect location."

"For what?" Orrin asked.

"For an ambush."

Orrin's eyes widened.

"We have a few more hours before daylight. The note says to be at the station at noon. We'll be there long before that," Waverly stated.

The sun was high in the sky when Orrin raised his hand and brought the others to a halt. "The station is just over that rise," he said, pointing to a long gradual slope that was dotted with rocks and scatterings of scrub. They dismounted and secured their horses in a thicket. Connors lifted his Henry from its scabbard, and Waverly fished his spyglass from his saddlebag. Slowly, they made their way up the rise on foot. When they were nearly at the crest, they sprawled out on the ground and low crawled the rest of the way.

The vista that stretched before them was a simple one. From their position, the land sloped down gradually until it flattened out for a distance of some half a mile. Then, it rose again slightly before its open contour was interrupted by a sparse collar of trees. Some one hundred fifty yards ahead loomed the old Pony Express station. It consisted of a long, low wooden structure, a sizable corral that was adjoined with a canopied one of a lesser size, several small outbuildings, and a number of hitching rails and water troughs. A stream flowed through the clearing, spilling over some large flat rocks before meandering off into some clusters of scrub in the distance. A thin braid of smoke snaked its way up from the chimney of the station before dissolving high into the sky above. Four saddled horses were secured to a hitching post in front of the station. Other than that, there was no sign of life in the vicinity.

"Four horses," Orrin whispered. "At least we won't be outnumbered. Let's move in."

Connors laid a restraining hand on Orrin's arm. "Not just yet, Orrin. Remember, they're expecting us."

Waverly trained the spyglass on the station for some time before swinging it slowly and deliberately from left to right across the entire clearing.

"What is it?" Orrin asked. "What are you looking for?"

"I'm looking for the spot where I would be if I wanted to ambush someone riding into the clearing."

"Anything?" Connors asked.

"Nothing. If they're dug in, they've picked an excellent position," Waverly said as he wiped his brow and rested his chin on his arm. "We'll have to move to the right a bit . . . change our angle."

They slid back down the slope and then circled to the right. From there, they edged their way back up. Again, Waverly worked the spyglass for a full minute. Finally, he lowered it and smiled.

"What is it?" Orrin asked anxiously.

"Over there, beyond that small cluster of rocks."

Orrin took the glass and peered intently at the spot Waverly had indicated. "I don't see anything."

"There's a rifle barrel jutting out just this side of that overhanging rock."

Orrin looked again and then grinned. "You're right, Captain. I see it now. You've got keen eyes."

"We're experienced in knowing where to look for such things." He took the spyglass and passed it to Chandler, who studied the location for some half a minute.

"They've picked a good spot. From there, they can control the ground in the front, rear, and one side of the station. They also have cover and concealment," Chandler said.

"Now, the question is—how many are in the station, and how many are in those rocks?" Connors asked.

"A good question, indeed. I think it's time we found out," Waverly said as he slipped a few feet back down the slope. "Sergeant Connors, the station is your responsibility. You can control it from here."

Connors nodded as he levered a cartridge into his Henry. "I think I'll mosey off this way a few more yards. I'll have a better angle at the door."

"Orrin . . . you, Lieutenant Chandler, and I will make our way in this direction in an effort to flank the ambushers."

Orrin nodded.

"We'll try to take them without firing any shots. Then, we can concentrate on the station without having to worry about being backshot," Waverly explained.

"Right," Orrin replied. He watched as Waverly and Chandler picked their way down the slope and then fell in behind them.

It took over ten minutes for them to work their way around to the rock cluster. At one point, they crawled on their bellies through scrub that was no more than a few feet high before they came to a position where they were able to see two men, some twenty feet away, well hidden from the clearing, ensconced amidst a scattering of rocks and some tall grass. Both men were resting on their sides, rifles cradled in their arms, their attention directed at the clearing below where the abandoned station lay.

Waverly nodded to Chandler, who rolled a few feet off to his right. Both of them trained their .44s on the pair who lay in ambush.

"Don't move a muscle." Waverly's words were even and deadly serious, and the two men seemed to sense the ominous tone his voice conveyed, for although they tensed in sudden surprise, they did not turn to face the man who spoke them. "Slowly, drop your rifles."

After a brief pause, both men did as they were ordered.

"Now, your gun belts."

One of the men complied, moving his hand slowly toward his buckle and loosening his gun belt from his waist. He then tossed it away.

"I ain't wearin' one," the other man said.

"All right, now, carefully back down the hill," Waverly directed, "and keep your hands where we can see them."

Both men turned and fixed their eyes on Waverly, Chandler, and Orrin. Scowling deeply, they complied with Waverly's command by holding their hands in the air as they slid down the slope on their sides. When they were out of any possible visual contact with the station, Waverly instructed them to stand. They got to their feet awkwardly, regarding Waverly coldly as they did so.

They were hardened, grizzled looking men with poor clothes. They wore beards, had long, shaggy hair, and were swarthy in appearance.

"Do you know them?" Waverly asked Orrin.

Orrin nodded. "I've seen them around. The one on the left is Jess Monroe. The other is his stepbrother, Tap Horner."

"How many are in the station house?" Waverly asked, training his .44 on them while Chandler patted them down for weapons.

"Just one," Jess Monroe replied. "Sam Eggars."

Chandler pulled a bowie knife out of Tap Horner's boot and tossed it into the grass. "What were you planning to do with this?"

Horner frowned at him bitterly.

"Where's my sister?" Orrin demanded.

The two men looked at each other. "We don't know nothin' about your sister," Monroe rapped.

"Liar!" Orrin took a step toward them, but Waverly restrained him.

"We're looking for Nora Stuart. The note told us that she was here . . . at the relay station," Waverly explained.

"We don't know nothin' about any note," Monroe replied.

"In that case, what are you doing out here?"

Monroe licked his lips and stared awkwardly at Waverly.

"We can read an ambush easily enough," Chandler put in.

"I tell you, we don't know nothin' about any note or any woman," Monroe reiterated.

Waverly nodded. "There are four horses in the corral below. Who rides the fourth one?"

Monroe and Horner looked at each other uneasily.

"It's . . . it's a pack horse," Monroe finally said.

"It's carrying a saddle," Waverly countered. "Now, I'll ask you again, how many are in the station house?"

Monroe lowered his eyes, and Horner glanced at him uncomfortably.

"All right. There are two—Sam Eggars and Ed Ringer. They're waitin' down there to waylay you while we were ready to catch you in a crossfire from up here."

"They're lying! Nora's in that station house!" Orrin uttered desperately.

"I tell you we're not. Eggars and Ringer are the only ones down there, and that's the plain and simple truth," Monroe avowed.

"It had better be . . . because your lives are going to depend on it," Waverly returned.

"We ain't lookin' to die, mister . . . not for no twenty-five a month," Horner chimed in.

Waverly considered them closely, half convinced that they were telling the truth. "Who gives you your orders?"

"Lynch," Monroe answered.

"Lynch . . . yes, we've met him. He doesn't look like the kind of man who could plan something like this. Who gives orders to Lynch?"

"Mr. Ludlow."

"Carl Ludlow?" Orrin asked in surprise.

"That's right," Monroe said.

"Exactly what were your orders?" Waverly asked.

"To kill the lot of you and bury your bodies out in the woods where nobody would find you."

"How were you to recognize us?" Waverly asked.

"We were told some men would be by the station at noon. We were to dry gulch 'em—pure and simple, but like I said before, we don't know nothin' about any woman."

"What about Dugger?"

The stepbrothers shot puzzled glances at each other.

"The boy who was dragged to his death," Chandler put in.

They did not respond, but the expressions on their faces told Waverly and Chandler that they were in the dark about the matter.

"All right, suppose you tell your friends inside the station house that we've got the drop on you. Will they come out without putting up a fight?" Waverly asked.

Monroe considered the question. "No. They'll try to save their own skins."

Waverly thought over the situation. "In that case, we'll have to trick them into coming out, and you're going to help us."

Monroe and Horner looked at each other nervously.

"We'll fire some shots in the air from your rifles. Then, you'll call to them. Tell them that you ambushed us . . . that you need their help in disposing of our bodies."

Monroe and Horner mulled over the plan. "It might work," Horner said.

"It had better," Waverly replied coldly. He turned to

Orrin. "Go back to our horses and get some rope. Tell Connors what we plan to do."

Orrin nodded, spun on his heels, and ran quickly down the slope. He returned in just over five minutes.

Waverly instructed him to take Horner further down the slope and tie him. Waverly then picked up one of the rifles and fired it in the air several times in rapid succession. He then waited a full minute before he directed Monroe to climb to the top of the rock cluster that he and Horner had occupied and call down to Eggars and Ringer.

In the meantime, Chandler worked his way to a position from which he could view the station house without being seen.

Monroe did as he was told, and less than a minute later, two men emerged from the station house.

"Me and Horner got 'em!" Monroe called out. "Come up and give us a hand."

A moment passed, and then Chandler turned and whispered over his shoulder to Waverly, "They're coming up."

Waverly then motioned Monroe back down the slope and directed Orrin to bind him and place him next to Horner. He quickly maneuvered his way back up the slope until he was some half a dozen yards from Chandler. Together, they waited for Eggars and Ringer to reach their position. Waverly peered between some rocks and saw the men for the first time. They wore handguns but carried no rifles. When they were some twenty feet from the top of the slope, Waverly nodded to Chandler, and the two of them rose to their feet, their .44s in their hands, barrels levelled at Eggars and Ringer. The two men were so startled at the unexpected sight of the men they had been sent to kill that they nearly stumbled back down the slope.

"Toss the guns aside, boys," Chandler said.

Reluctantly, each man did as he was told and then raised his hands.

"Keep on climbing," Chandler said, waving his .44 in a circular motion.

They did as ordered. They were nearly at the crest when one of them slipped, fell to his knees, and landed on his side. He started to rise to his feet, but as he did so, his hand moved under his coat and came out holding a small handgun.

Chandler let loose with a shot from his .44, striking the man's hand and sending the gun flying through the air.

The man clutched his wrist and grimaced in pain as he stared up at Chandler with a venomous glare.

When the two men reached the crest, Orrin was ready with another rope.

Chandler remained behind to stand guard over the four would-be ambushers while Waverly and Orrin descended the slope toward the station house. They moved hastily, their guns in their hands in the event that there might be others about, but they met no resistance. The door to the station house was open, and they entered cautiously.

"Nora?" Orrin called out. "Nora, where are you?"

There was no reply. The station house was empty, and there was no sign that Nora had ever been there. A few sticks of furniture layered with dust were all that remained of what must have been a once thriving business venture. Some cigarette stubs left on the floor and a small fire burning itself out in the hearth were the only signs of any recent inhabitants.

"Monroe was telling the truth. Nora isn't here," Orrin concluded glumly. "What do we do now?"

"We find out where she is and we go after her," Waverly replied. He turned on his heel and stepped outside. Orrin followed. It was then that a rifle shot rang out, filling the air with a reverberating sound that seemed to carry for miles. Waverly spun about and lurched toward the station house door, pulling Orrin after him. Here, they remained under cover, moving to the windows of the station house, from which they scanned the slopes around them for any movement. Five minutes later, they spotted a man walking toward them, one arm raised in the air while the other dangled at his side. Connors strolled behind him, training his Henry on the man.

Waverly and Orrin stepped outside and moved in their direction. They met about fifty feet from the station house.

"Another prisoner, Captain," Connors announced.

"I'm hurt. I need a doctor," the man moaned. He was similar in appearance to Monroe and Horner, with disheveled clothes and a threatening look. His coat, in particular, was ragged and had a hole in the sleeve. A trail of blood was trickling from the hole.

"You know him?" Waverly asked.

"No," Orrin replied.

"Shortly after Orrin told me what you were planning, I heard a horse whinny from off in that direction," Connors said, jerking his thumb over his shoulder. "I checked it out . . . discovered this hombre in some tall grass, drawing a bead on you and Orrin. I figure I winged him just in time."

"So there was a fifth man for insurance. Well, they

almost collected on their policy but not quite," Waverly mused. Turning his attention to Connors' prisoner, he asked, "What's your name?"

"I need a doctor."

"The captain asked you a question," Connors said, prodding the man with the barrel of his Henry.

"Gibbs," the man answered.

Waverly nodded. He questioned Gibbs about Nora, but he appeared to know no more than the fact that he was hired, along with the others, to ambush some men.

"All right, we'll collect the others and head back to town. We'll take them to your place, Orrin, until we can decide how to approach this matter in the way that places Nora in the least possible peril."

Chapter Thirteen

When they were a few miles from the Stuart house, Waverly rode up alongside Monroe's horse.

Monroe looked up at him askance.

"When your job was done and you were to have buried us, where were you supposed to report?" Waverly asked.

"We were to report to Lynch . . . at Mr. Ludlow's house."

"Besides Lynch, how many men are there on Ludlow's spread?"

"Why should I tell you anything? I'm goin' to jail anyway."

"Because the life of an innocent girl may hang in the balance," Waverly said.

"I told you before—we don't know nothin' about any girl."

"Let's say that I believe you . . . but after you were sent to that relay station to dry gulch us, a young boy was killed and a girl was abducted from her home. You want that on your conscience?"

Monroe eyed Waverly narrowly. Finally, he said, "No. I want no part of harmin' a girl."

"Then, tell me how many men we can expect to encounter at Ludlow's."

Monroe contemplated the question. "Besides Lynch, there will be two or three others—no more. Most of his men are haulin' freight or off doin' other chores."

"If you're lying to me, I'll come back and put a hole in you," Waverly said, his eyes locked on Monroe's.

"I ain't lyin', mister. I know when I'm hogtied."

Waverly considered him for a long moment before riding over to Orrin.

"Orrin, is the sheriff of St. Jo a man you can count on?"

"He is, but he's out of town . . . won't be back until next week. Joe Storm is his chief deputy, and he's a friend of mine. He's a good man."

"All right. I think it best that you ride into town ahead of us and contact Joe Storm. Tell him what has happened and bring him out to your place. We'll keep this lot in your barn in the meantime."

"What if I should run into Lynch?" Orrin asked, an expression of fear commingled with anger written on his face.

"I'm gambling that he won't be there, but if he is, it's best that he sees you alone and not the rest of us."

"All right." Orrin lashed his horse and rode ahead.

Joe Storm was six-foot-three, broad-shouldered, and lean at the waist. He was about thirty, mustached, with eyes that were quick and alert. He carried a .44 holstered low and gave the impression that he was skilled in its use. He brought two fellow deputies along to round up the prisoners. After shaking hands with

Waverly, Chandler, and Connors, he stood with his arms folded and regarded them seriously. "Orrin gave me the lowdown. I'll have this pack of rats in a cell in no time. Now, as to Nora, Orrin tells me that Ludlow and Lynch are behind her disappearance."

Waverly nodded. "It appears that way."

"Lynch is a hard one. He's been involved in a few scrapes, but nothin' worth bein' jailed over. He's mighty fast with a gun, and most men won't cross his path," Storm explained.

"We've seen him in town," Connors said.

"As far as Mr. Ludlow's concerned, he's one of the most important businessmen we have in St. Jo. He's respected, as most men with money are. He's always kept to himself. Most folks don't know much about him and don't care. That's the way of the West. He's never broken the law, but he does employ some hardcases who haul his freight. I don't have to tell you about the likes of them."

"This Ludlow . . . exactly what does he look like?" Chandler asked.

"Well, he's about thirty, your size, with broad shoulders. He wears expensive suits."

"Does he have a beard?"

"Yes."

Waverly, Chandler, and Connors glanced at each other.

"Orrin told me about this Rebel officer named Traxler and the pain he caused you during the war. Do you think he and Ludlow are one and the same?"

"Could be, Deputy," Connors replied. "One way or the other, we aim to find out."

"I'm mighty sorry about what happened to the lot of you. Orrin tells me you're fine men. But right now, Miss

Nora Stuart is the most important thing on my mind.
Do we understand each other?" Storm asked, eyeing
them closely.

"We do," Waverly returned, "and I can assure you
that she's also the most important thing on my mind."

Storm nodded as he digested Waverly's words. "I
look forward to your help, and I reckon I couldn't turn
it down if I wanted to."

"That's right enough, Deputy, you couldn't,"
Connors put in.

"Just so we get the rules straight . . . this matter is
goin' to be handled legal and proper. If you ride with
me, you ride by my orders. We do everything possible
to get Nora back. If these men choose to surrender to
the law, they'll be given that chance. If they decide to
throw down on us, that's another matter."

"We can live with that," Chandler said.

"I'm glad to hear it. If Mr. Ludlow proves to be this
man Traxler, he'll answer to the authorities for what
he's done."

"Just how do you plan to handle this matter,
Deputy?" Waverly inquired.

"The way I handle every matter—head on. We ride
out to Mr. Ludlow's spread and we confront him. If
Nora's there, we take her. If there's any resistance, we
put an end to it right then and there."

"You're a mighty direct man, Deputy," Connors
replied.

"I represent the law, and the law always takes the
shortest and most direct path."

Waverly ran his hand across his chin. "I like the way
you approach matters, Deputy, but don't you think that
a frontal maneuver such as that might put Nora's life at
risk?"

"On the contrary. If we lay our cards on the table, it should show the people we're dealing with that they've been found out and there's nowhere to run and hide."

Waverly's facial muscles tightened as he mulled over Storm's strategy.

Sensing Waverly's doubts, Storm said, "I know that you wouldn't want us to do anything that would put Nora in any more danger. Neither would I, but you have to realize one thing. Mr. Ludlow is an important man around here. We still don't know exactly how he's involved in this matter. He may be this man Traxler. Then again, he may not be. So far, all we have that connects him to Nora's disappearance is the word of these bushwhackers."

Orrin stepped toward Storm. "And the fact that Lynch is involved."

"Yeah, but that, in itself, doesn't prove Mr. Ludlow's guilt. I can't very well go ridin' out to his spread, shootin' up the place without direct proof of his involvement. Why, we don't even know if Nora's there."

"But, Joe—"

"He's right, Orrin," Waverly interrupted. "So far, all we have are suspicions. We haven't even set eyes on Ludlow yet."

Orrin nodded as he hung his head.

"I'm glad we're in accord," Storm said.

"We are, Deputy, but that doesn't mean that we can't take out some insurance," Waverly said.

Storm eyed him narrowly.

"We're ex-soldiers. We still haven't gotten soldiering completely out of our blood. I guess maybe we never will. We like to know the lay of the land—especially if it may prove to be the future sight of a battlefield. Now, suppose you describe Ludlow's spread to us," Waverly said, a half-smile on his face.

Storm grinned. He picked up a twig, hunkered down, and started to make marks in the dirt.

An hour later, Deputy Joe Storm and Orrin Stuart rode onto Carl Ludlow's spread. His ranch house was a two-story wooden structure with neatly painted shutters. The house was encircled on three sides by a wooden porch adorned with hanging plants and several chairs. A tidy arrangement of shrubbery fringed the porch along the entire length of the front of the house and continued around each side. There was a hitching rail just to the right of the front of the house, where a pair of horses was tied. Further off to the right were a barn and a large corral, home to some half a dozen horses that meandered about in an idle fashion. Their ears pricked up and one of them nickered as Storm and Orrin made their slow way down a path that led to the main house. Just beyond and slightly off to the right of the barn was a bunkhouse. There was no one about with the exception of one man who suddenly walked from around the side of the main house and strolled casually across the porch. Storm and Orrin reined in their horses just a few feet from the steps that led up to the front porch. It was then that Orrin recognized the man as Lynch. His skin began to crawl as he watched the freighter sidle along the porch until he stood beside one of the posts, around which he folded his left hand while his right fell in a smooth, slow arc toward the gun on his hip.

"We're lookin' for Mr. Ludlow," Storm announced, his eyes sizing up Lynch as he rested his hands on his saddle horn.

Lynch half grinned and half sneered as he stared at Storm and Orrin for a long time.

Orrin thought that Lynch appeared to be a bit surprised at seeing him.

"Mr. Ludlow is busy. He won't be seein' anybody today, Deputy."

"He'll be seein' us, and he'll be seein' us now," Storm returned, regarding Lynch with his dark gray eyes.

Lynch seemed taken aback by Storm's sharp response, but he remained adamant. "I usually handle Mr. Ludlow's chores, Deputy. Maybe I can help you."

"It's Mr. Ludlow we need to see," Storm replied.

"As I said, he's a mite busy now. Tomorrow'll have to do."

"Tomorrow won't do at all, Lynch," Orrin put in.

"Oh, and just what business have you got here, Stuart?"

"My sister."

"Your sister? I don't know anything about your sister other than to say that she's a pretty one," Lynch said through stained teeth.

"Why, you—" Orrin started to dismount, but Storm laid a restraining hand on his arm.

Lynch sneered again and tilted his head toward the bunkhouse. "You boys had best take a look before you start somethin' that you can't finish."

Orrin glanced at Storm. They turned and saw three men standing in front of the bunkhouse. Two were armed with handguns. The third held a rifle.

"Are you standin' against the law?" Storm asked.

"Oh, no, I wouldn't do that. I'm just here to protect Mr. Ludlow's interests, is all."

"And just what is it that Mr. Ludlow has to fear?" Storm returned.

"Why, nothin', Deputy. It's just that he's a busy man, is all."

"Then, what is it that you have to fear, Lynch?" Orrin asked.

"Me . . . I've done nothin' wrong."

"Then, tell me where my sister is."

"Like I said . . . I don't know anything about your sister."

"Last night you told Stuart here and some other men that one of their friends had an accident and that he could be found at Stuart's house. When they got there, their friend was there all right—dead."

"Deputy, I don't know what Stuart here has been tellin' you, but I flat out deny it."

"You're a liar, Lynch!" Orrin barked angrily. "What about the note concerning my sister that was left at my place?"

Lynch shrugged. "It's his word against mine, Deputy. That is, unless his friends are here to back up his story, and I don't see any of 'em," Lynch returned, a smug expression on his face.

"His friends are here, Lynch. You just haven't looked in the right places."

Lynch turned suddenly. His jaw dropped when he saw Chandler standing at the end of the porch, his hand poised next to his holster.

It was then that Chandler saw the pendant with the red stone dangling from a silver chain that hung from Lynch's neck. Chandler's fist clenched in hate as he thought of Dugger, but control and intent overrode his emotions, and he remembered his reason for being here. "Your plan backfired, Lynch. The ambush failed, and your men talked. They talked very freely, and they implicated you," he announced.

Lynch's lips twitched as his head swiveled from Chandler to Storm. "You're still outnumbered," he said. "It's four to three, and we can bury the lot of you right here."

"You don't plan very well, Lynch. You don't count well either." It was Waverly's voice.

Lynch turned again, as did the three men by the bunkhouse. They saw Waverly and Connors standing near the barn. Waverly's .44 was under his belt, and his hand was resting on the grip. Connors had his Henry leveled at the nearest man.

The men near the bunkhouse looked at each other uneasily as their once comfortable odds had suddenly plummeted.

"Throw down your gun, or make your play," Chandler said flatly.

Lynch turned toward Chandler, stood with his legs slightly apart, and sized up the one-armed man who faced him from just ten feet away. Chandler's resolve was solid, and his gun hand seemed all too comfortable as it hung next to his .44. Lynch hesitated for a long moment, suddenly uncertain of himself. His fingers twitched nervously against the side of his holster as he contemplated making his move.

Chandler held his ground, his eyes locked on Lynch's, his focus unbroken as though he were staring down a long, straight tunnel.

When Lynch finally made up his mind, he moved quickly. His hand came up swiftly, clutching the handle of his gun and pulling it from its holster. His speed as a fast draw, however, was no match for Chandler's. Chandler drew and fired twice before Lynch could even level his gun barrel at his opponent. Both shots struck Lynch in the chest, knocking him backward against a post. He tottered there for a second and then fell over the porch rail and landed in a heap on the ground.

An instant after Lynch had drawn his weapon, the men near the bunkhouse made their move. Waverly drew and fired, and Connors cut loose with his Henry. One of the men by the bunkhouse stood uneasily, clutching his arm. The one holding the rifle lay on the ground. The third tossed his gun aside and raised his hands.

Storm had pulled his gun and leveled it at the two men still standing. "Just stand where you are, boys, and keep your hands where I can see 'em."

Waverly and Connors moved toward them quickly and collected their weapons.

"This one's still alive, Deputy, but he's going to need a doctor," Connors said as he knelt beside the man he had shot.

"We'll get him tended to right off," Storm announced.

Orrin leaped from his horse and strode onto the porch. "Joe, if Nora's been hurt in any way—"

"Stand easy, Orrin. I haven't forgotten about Nora." Storm climbed down from his saddle and followed at Orrin's heels.

"There won't be any need for guns, gentlemen. I won't resist," a voice said from within the house. Suddenly, the front door opened, and a man stepped out onto the porch.

Waverly and Connors looked up. Chandler eyed him closely. The three veterans glanced at each other and then fixed their gaze on the man.

"Is this Carl Ludlow?" Waverly asked Storm.

Storm nodded. "It is. Is he the man you know as Traxler?"

Waverly slid his .44 back under his belt. Regarding Ludlow narrowly, he said, "No. I've never seen this man before."

Chapter Fourteen

Carl Ludlow stood on the porch with his shoulders hung low. A grave look covered his face. "I don't know exactly what's going on, but I've got a pretty good idea."

"Keep talkin', Mr. Ludlow," Storm urged.

"I overheard your conversation with Lynch when you rode up, Deputy. I believe the man you want is Mel Garver."

"Garver . . . your bookkeeper?" Storm asked, puzzled.

"He's not really my bookkeeper. In fact, it would be closer to the truth if I told you that it was the other way around."

Storm pushed back his Stetson and scratched his head.

"I can explain everything later, Deputy. Right now, I believe that this young man is looking for his sister," Ludlow stated.

"That's right. What do you know about her, Ludlow?" Orrin pressed.

"I haven't seen her. At least, she hasn't been here, but

I believe I know where she's been taken. I overheard Garver talking to Lynch earlier. He told Lynch that he was going to take the woman to the cabin. That could mean only one place—the old trapper's cabin near the western perimeter of this spread. Garver goes there sometimes when he wants to be alone."

Storm eyed Orrin uneasily and then turned to Waverly, Chandler, and Connors. "I know the place. It's in the bogs."

"The bogs?" Chandler asked.

"The quicksand bogs. Nobody ever goes there. A crazy trapper built that cabin over ten years ago. He didn't want anybody around, and he got his wish. That land isn't fit for man or beast. More than one steer has wandered into those bogs and never come out. There's even talk that an entire covered wagon once went down with several passengers on board. Of course, no one can prove that story."

"There's a trail that leads to that cabin," Ludlow said, "but I don't know where it is. I've never actually seen the place. I don't know how Garver ever found his way in."

"He's killed her! He's killed Nora and hidden her body in the quicksand!" Orrin burst out.

"Steady, Orrin," Waverly said.

"I don't think so," Ludlow interceded.

The others all regarded Ludlow intently.

"I don't know why Garver took your sister, but I can only guess that it was as a bargaining chip. Garver is a careful man. He wouldn't throw away any edge that he might have."

"That makes sense, Orrin," Storm added.

"Yes, but he will kill Nora once he thinks he's done away with us. He has no other choice," Waverly put in.

"That's true," Ludlow said, "but you may still have a chance to save the woman."

"What do you mean?" Orrin asked, a tone of desperation in his voice.

"Well, whatever it is that Garver has done, he's protected himself with every step he's taken. I overheard him tell Lynch that when the job was done, Lynch was to report to him at the cabin. I'm certain that Garver would do no harm to the woman until he knew for sure that he held all the cards," Ludlow explained.

"Then, Lynch knew the way to the cabin," Storm said.

"Unfortunately, Lynch isn't about to tell us anything," Chandler added.

They turned toward Lynch's crumpled form lying just below the porch rail.

Waverly strode over to Lynch's body, bent over it, and picked up the gunman's Stetson. He held it for some time, contemplating it as he turned it over in his hands.

The sun was low in the sky, and the shadows began to stretch across the land like ink spilling into a thin carpet. The few remaining patches of clouds were nothing more than blurs against a background of darkening blue. Connors, Chandler, and Waverly sat in their saddles beside Storm and Orrin. They had reined in their horses at the edge of a thick stand of oaks as Waverly studied the terrain ahead through his spyglass. It was a flat, lonely expanse of ground—grayish brown in color, yet appearing bleaker under the spreading darkness. Occasional clusters of tall reeds suggested marshland, but no other vegetation or life form manifested itself for better than a mile. The cabin lay about four hundred yards ahead—a plain looking structure with a thin line of smoke snaking its way out of a rock chimney.

"I don't see any horses. They must be tied on the other side of the cabin. I can't make out any trail either," Waverly said.

"I wish that I could help you, Captain, but the truth of the matter is that I don't know the way in myself. I never knew anybody that did," Storm replied.

"Lynch had to know," Connors said.

"Yeah," Waverly said dejectedly as he passed the spyglass to Chandler.

"And if you don't know the right way in, Traxler's going to know it right away," Chandler added.

"If I can't find the right way in, I won't have to worry about Traxler. I'll end up at the bottom of the quicksand."

"I don't much like your chances, Captain," Connors said.

"I don't either, but I am riding Lynch's horse. Maybe if I give him his head, he'll take me in."

"I wouldn't give odds," Chandler returned.

Waverly frowned. "No, neither would I."

"A light just went on in the cabin," Chandler announced, passing the spyglass to Orrin.

The others focused their attention on the single window visible from their angle. They could see a soft glow, the only sign of life in an otherwise forlorn tract of land.

"He's there, all right," Connors said.

"I'm going to have to move in now. In a matter of minutes, it may be too dark for you to follow me." Waverly checked his appearance. He was wearing Lynch's clothes, gun, and gun belt. "In this failing light, I may be able to get close enough to make a play against Traxler before he realizes that I'm not Lynch."

"Good luck, Captain," Connors said.

"Watch yourself," Storm added. "I'm not havin' much confidence that this will work, but I'm blamed if I can think of a better idea."

Waverly urged Lynch's horse forward, and the animal moved ahead. The horse, a sturdy buckskin, picked up its feet readily and, for some fifty or sixty yards, seemed to know instinctively the trail toward the cabin. Then, something went wrong. The horse nickered uneasily and tossed its head to and fro as if sensing that danger lay ahead. Waverly coaxed it forward, but the animal paid little attention as it backed away and half reared into the air. Waverly remained adamant, however, patting the horse's neck and speaking to it softly. Finally, the horse moved ahead reluctantly, obviously uncomfortable with its situation and ready to bolt at any moment. It moved with tentative steps for another fifty yards before its front legs faltered as it sank into morass halfway up to its knees. It whinnied loudly, allowing panic to usurp its reason. Waverly immediately leaped from the saddle and tugged at the reins, doing his best to help the frightened animal to extricate itself from the disappearing footing that surrounded them. Together, after some doing, horse and man were able to retrace their steps and return to firmer ground. The horse, still severely frightened, would have no more of this and refused to advance, despite Waverly's efforts to quiet it. Waverly knew he would have to continue on foot, for the poor beast could no more pick its way across this quagmire than it could fly through the clouds.

Waverly started out on his own, choosing a different angle from which to approach the cabin. Sheer trial and error, retracing his steps, and changing directions some half a dozen times brought him to within a hundred twenty yards of the cabin. It was growing dark, however, and he knew that the others, who were watching his progress, would soon lose sight of him in the failing light. He decided that he had to gamble. Cupping his hands to his mouth, he faced the cabin and called out, "Garver!"

There was no response.

He repeated the name several more times before a shadow of a figure emerged from the cabin and stood beside it.

"Lynch?" a voice sang out.

"Yeah."

"Why don't you come ahead?" the voice called, a ring of suspicion in it.

"Can't. I'm hurt. Need help," Waverly shouted back, hoping that the distance between them would serve to disguise his voice.

There was a long pause, and then the figure advanced, moving in a circuitous path that brought him to within twenty yards of Waverly.

Waverly dropped to his knees and hung his head low so that the approaching man would not be able to recognize him. Another full minute passed, for the man was, no doubt, searching the landscape around him for any unexpected visitors. Apparently satisfied, he moved on toward Waverly.

Waverly leaned forward until he was on all fours, feigning an injury in an effort to avert making eye contact with the man. He could only hope that Lynch's clothes and the fading light might do the trick—at least until he could gain admission to the cabin.

He felt an arm wrap around his chest and help him to his feet, but he deliberately continued to hang his head low so that his face was out of view.

"Your clothes . . . they're covered with blood. You've been wounded!" the voice said.

"Hurt . . . bad," Waverly moaned in the hoarsest tone he could muster.

"Then, the ambush at the relay station—it failed?"

"No . . . only one survived. I saw to him . . . dead . . . now," Waverly whispered, "but he got me too."

"I'll get you to the cabin . . . have a look at you," the voice came back.

Waverly half walked, half stumbled to exaggerate his pretended condition as the man supported him and helped him to negotiate the remaining steps that brought them to the cabin. As the man brushed against him, Waverly felt a handgun just under the man's arm . . . a shoulder holster, he guessed. Waverly dared not look up and only watched the ground before them as they lumbered clumsily along until he could see a flood of light at their feet, coming from what must have been a lamp from within the cabin. The door was open and he felt wooden floorboards under his feet as he was assisted inside. He was half dragged toward a bunk, where the man turned him around and maneuvered him into a position whereby he could be stretched out onto a mattress. Waverly knew that he had to act now. In one swift motion, he shoved the man away from him and drew his .44. As he looked up, he saw the man stagger backward until he struck the wall of the cabin. Waverly rose to his feet and trained his gun on a man who wore one of the most startled expressions he had ever seen. In height and build, he was a match for Waverly. He was clean shaven, wore wire-rimmed spectacles, and a pinstriped suit. His dark eyes bored into Waverly as though they were brands, burned black from heat.

"Waverly . . ." he said in a voice that was barely above a whisper.

"Traxler . . ." Waverly said through gritted teeth as he stared at the man with a hatred he held for no other save the Devil himself. He raised the .44 and pointed it at Traxler's face.

"John . . . no!"

Waverly froze. He glanced to his right and saw Nora seated in a chair, her hands bound behind her.

"Nora—are you all right?" he asked.

"I'm all right," she said. "I'm all right!"

"Waverly . . . I left you for dead once—you and the others. I should've made sure," he sneered.

"I guess a man can crawl back from hell if he has to, Traxler."

"Those clothes . . . then, Lynch is dead?"

Waverly nodded. "Lynch failed, as did all the others. You're through, Traxler. Your entire outfit is through, and you're going to die for your sins. I only regret that a man like you can only die once." He raised the .44 again.

"No, John, you can't!" Nora screamed.

Waverly fired several times. The sound of the discharged gun was deafening within the small structure, and for a long moment, life within the cabin seemed suspended.

Nora stared at Waverly in shock.

Waverly still held the gun loosely in his hand.

Traxler stood motionless, his mouth open in frozen terror. The wall behind him was riddled with bullet holes that outlined his head.

It took only a matter of minutes for the others to burst into the cabin. Chandler and Connors came through the door first, their guns raised, followed by Storm and Orrin. By this time, Waverly had loosened the ropes that bound Nora and she was standing beside him, enfolded in his arm. When she saw Orrin, she reached out and drew him to her, tears flowing freely as she kissed her brother's cheek again and again.

"Shoulder holster," Waverly said, nodding toward Traxler.

Connors stepped over, patted down Traxler, and quickly found the hidden weapon. He passed it to Storm, who tucked it under his belt and then considered the scene within the cabin.

"Are you all right, Miss Stuart?" he asked.

"I'm fine now, Deputy," Nora returned, managing a wide smile of relief.

"I'm mighty glad to hear it. We were all growin' concerned." He then turned to Traxler. "Well, gents, is Mr. Garver here the man from your past?"

"He is," Chandler replied. "His name is Traxler. He's an ex-Confederate lieutenant, and no worse butcher ever lived."

Storm nodded. "There'll be an extensive investigation. The law will see that the appropriate punishment is meted out."

"There's no punishment on this earth that's fit for a man like him," Connors shot back as he glared at Traxler with a hatred that coursed through his body like poison.

Traxler's mouth tightened, but he did not speak.

"What happened to Dugger?" Waverly asked.

Traxler sneered.

Connors stepped forward and backhanded him across the face.

Traxler's head snapped backward, and a trickle of

blood oozed down his lip. "If you mean the corporal . . . he recognized me on the street. I have to admit, I was just as surprised to see him as he must have been to see me. He confronted me. A few of my men were with me. We were able to overpower him. It wasn't easy. He put up quite a fight."

"What did you do to him?" Chandler asked.

"Does it matter now?"

"It matters," Connors replied. "It always matters how a man dies."

"I had him dragged behind a horse."

"Why? Why did you have to do that to him?" Chandler asked. "Didn't he suffer enough by your hand?"

"I realized that if he was alive, then some of you might be as well. You might be together, and obviously you could pose a threat to me. I questioned him about it, but he wouldn't talk. I needed answers, and torturing him was the only way to get them."

"You're an expert at torture, aren't you, Traxler?" Waverly said.

"I was a soldier. That was war."

"You were never a soldier. You just wore a uniform," Waverly rapped bitterly. "We fought Confederates we respected, but you deserve nothing but a rope for what you did. You may wear clothes and walk on your uprights, but you're an animal."

Traxler listened to Waverly's words, but his expression did not change.

"Why did you kidnap my sister?" Orrin asked.

"The corporal died without talking, but one of my men happened to notice the two of you together. Grabbing your sister gave me the leverage I needed to learn if there were any other ex-soldiers who might be nearby, and it served to keep the law out of the way."

"Murder and kidnapping are hanging offenses," Storm announced. "Those are within my jurisdiction, but under the circumstances, I'll let the federal authorities decide who gets you and what sentence you draw. Let's get him to a jail cell, boys, and let's see that Miss Stuart here is taken care of."

Storm took Traxler by the arm and led him from the cabin.

Connors picked up an oil lamp from a small table and carried it outside. Chandler walked beside him while Nora made her way between Waverly and Orrin.

It was dark now, and the ground looked like a gray blanket covered with streaks of black.

"Watch your step," Storm cautioned. "We were able to drop some stones along your path when we followed you in, Captain Waverly, but it's pretty bleak out here now."

"If we move slowly, we shouldn't have any trouble," Connors added as he held the lamp high in the air.

The group picked their way carefully through the bog, stepping gingerly over ground that could suck them under within a matter of seconds. Connors was able to locate a series of small stones that he and the others had placed along the track taken by Waverly and Traxler. It was slow going, made more difficult by the gathering darkness, but they made progress and were soon nearly two hundred yards from their horses. It was then that Traxler halted dead in his tracks.

The others pulled up and eyed him narrowly.

"Keep movin', Traxler," Storm ordered.

"I don't think so, Deputy." His words were cold and almost without life.

Storm trained his gun on Traxler, and Chandler did the same.

"Those guns don't mean anything to me. I know that I'm a dead man. It's only a matter of time."

They regarded him with little feeling.

"Yet there may be another road for me," Traxler said as he turned and faced them.

"What are you gettin' at?" Storm asked.

Traxler did not reply; instead, he pointed into the darkness. "The quicksand."

Chandler and Connors glanced at each other as did Waverly and Nora.

"A long imprisonment, a trial, an execution . . . it won't do."

"That's the fate you designed for yourself," Waverly said.

Traxler looked at the faces of the ex-soldiers who stood before him. "You said that I tortured you, and that's true enough—I did, but wouldn't you be doing the same to me by putting me through all that? Wouldn't you be there all the while . . . watching me through prison bars . . . counting the steps I'd take on the scaffold . . . watching me swing from a rope?"

"Traxler, you've got nothing to say about the way you leave this earth. That was taken out of your hands a long time ago," Waverly countered.

"Oh, but I have, Captain." With that, he shoved Storm aside and leaped off the path.

Chandler raised his gun, but Waverly placed a restraining hand on his arm.

They watched in astonishment as Traxler ran into the darkness.

Connors followed, holding the lamp over his head, but he soon lost his footing and began to stumble. Storm caught his arm and held him firmly, for he had already sunk into morass up to his knees. Chandler was on the scene in an instant, and between the two of them, they were able to pull Connors back to firmer ground.

The others caught up and stood beside them, peering into the darkness.

Once again, Connors raised the lamp high over his head. It was then that they were able to see Traxler, not ten feet away. He was mired up to his waist. His arms were outspread as though he were treading water. He twisted at first, in an instinctive attempt to recapture secure footing, but instead, he sank deeper and deeper . . . until the murky, muddy ooze rose to his chest. For some time, he remained in this position, as though he was suspended between life and the near darkness of a world known only to the dead. He did not speak, his eyes did not seem to focus; he merely existed in this state, awaiting the inevitable departure from existence as he knew it.

"I'll go for a rope!" Chandler called out. He started to move, but his legs seemed anchored to the ground as he saw Traxler suddenly slip even further into the bog, and Chandler knew that there was nothing that he or anyone else could do.

With trembling fingers, Traxler tore the spectacles from his face. He looked upward into the night sky, a sardonic expression on his face as the ooze reached his chin. His mouth opened and closed several times as if to gasp for air, but each time more ooze flowed over his lips. He choked and then coughed and then completely slid from view, leaving only a shallow depression that was soon filled in by more shifting sand and ooze. In a matter of seconds, there was no longer any visible trace of his existence other than a gathering of bubbles that quickly dissolved, and a ripple within the mire that disappeared into the darkness.

Chapter Fifteen

They buried Dugger the following afternoon. A priest performed the ceremony and said some kind words over the fallen corporal. Besides Orrin and Nora, Deputy Joe Storm was the only other person present to offer condolences to Waverly, Chandler, and Connors. After they left the cemetery, they returned to the Stuart home, where Nora served them all coffee.

"He was a good boy," Connors recalled, moisture forming in his eye. "He had so much more of life to learn and enjoy."

"He survived several skirmishes while he was wearing the uniform. He shouldn't have had to die the way he did. That was no way for any soldier to go . . . it was no way for any man to go," Chandler added.

Waverly reflected back over the time he had known Dugger. There were things that he wanted to say, but he could not bring himself to say them.

They sat in comparative silence for some time as one or another attempted to make small talk, but the general feeling in the room was one of deep sorrow and personal loss. Finally, after a time, Storm rose to his feet.

"I've got to be headin' back to the office. Carl Ludlow will be in in about an hour. I know that you boys will want to learn what light he can shed on this matter."

"We'll be there, Deputy," Waverly replied.

Storm nodded. "Once again, I'm sorry about your friend."

"We appreciate it," Waverly said.

After Storm left, Nora refilled everyone's cup and then sat down next to Waverly. "What will you boys be doing with yourselves now?" she asked, her lips twitching slightly.

"We haven't given it much thought. We're in no hurry to move on," Waverly said.

She nodded.

Chandler placed his cup on a side table. "Now that Traxler is gone and his hired thugs are dead or behind bars, you and Orrin may be able to resurrect your freight line."

Orrin's eyes widened. "Why, that's true enough. Nora, that means we may be able to stay on here in St. Jo."

Nora beamed. "Oh, Orrin, I can only hope that that's so."

Turning to the others, Orrin said, "I could use some help . . . good men who know horses and can work as drivers."

"I don't see why we can't stick around and lend a hand for a while, Captain," Connors said.

Waverly glanced at Chandler, who nodded. "Then, I guess we're your men," Waverly said with a smile.

Nora turned away so as not to reveal her happiness.

"I'll get some more coffee," she announced as she started for the kitchen.

The others looked after her, and then Chandler and Connors glanced at Waverly, who cleared his throat.

A few minutes later they heard the sound of a buggy approaching. There was a knock at the door, and Orrin answered it. They heard the soft voice of a woman ask for Dell Chandler.

Chandler looked up in surprise. He stood up immediately and strode to the door. He was stunned to see Marion standing on the porch, her hands clasped in front of her, her eyes wide with anxiety.

"Marion." Chandler pronounced her name as though the word were a precious jewel.

"Dell . . . I came to speak to you. Is it all right?" she asked hesitantly.

For a long moment, he stared at her as though he did not believe that she was standing before him. Then, slowly, he nodded. He stepped onto the porch, took her arm, and led her away from the house.

"When we last talked, you mentioned that you would be visiting a family in St. Jo by the name of Stuart. I inquired in town where their house was. I was fortunate to find you here."

"We were . . . talking about Dugger."

"The young soldier who served with you?"

He nodded.

"How is he doing?"

"He's dead, Marion. He was murdered."

She pressed her hands to her mouth in shock. "I'm so sorry."

"The men responsible are also dead or in custody. We just returned from his funeral."

"How awful."

"Here in St. Jo, we met up with Traxler, the Confederate officer who tortured us in that prisoner of war camp. He's dead too."

Marion stared at him in shocked surprise. "Here? He was living here?"

"Yes, under another name. He took his own life. I'll tell you all about it later, but why have you come here?"

She peered into his eyes as though she were searching for something but was afraid to find it. "I thought over what you said when we last talked. I thought how brave a man you were and how brave you're going to have to be to go on with the way things are. I . . . I must have sounded very selfish to you."

"No, you sounded truthful. I didn't hold anything against you."

"I won't lie to you now and tell you that I'm not afraid. I am. I've never considered myself strong, but sometimes a man and wife have to find courage in each other. What I'm trying to say is that I'd like to know if you still want me . . . because if you do, I'll stand beside you wherever you go and whatever you do."

"It won't be easy, Marion, being saddled to a cripple."

"Maybe I was the cripple, Dell. Maybe the two of us can take turns leaning on each other . . . that is, if there's still a chance."

Their eyes locked as they stood side by side, and then Chandler pulled her toward him and held her closely.

Carl Ludlow sat on a straight-backed wooden chair in the jailhouse. Deputy Joe Storm sat behind a long walnut desk that was littered with correspondence and dodgers. Waverly occupied a chair facing Ludlow while Chandler and Connors stood nearby.

"I first met Mel Garver . . . or should I say . . . Traxler . . . nearly a year ago. We were on a stage bound for St. Jo when we struck up a conversation. I was a bookkeeper by profession back in Albany and decided to come west to broaden my prospects. I told him a little about myself, and he seemed more than just casually interested. He was a bit close-mouthed about himself at first, but it was a long trip, and he finally opened up. He told me that he came from a wealthy Southern family and that he had had a rift with his father and brother over the way their steamship business should be operated. He went on to explain that he had secretly taken his share of the family fortune and fled, with the intention of starting his own business and being his own boss. At that point in our conversation, he opened the valise on the seat beside him and tilted it so that I could look inside. It was loaded with currency. He said that it contained fifty thousand dollars.

Despite the fact that he considered the sum his rightful share, he felt that he had placed himself in a questionable legal position, and he feared that it was an absolute certainty that his father and brother would have the law on his trail. For this reason, he had seen fit to change his identity and leave the state. He opted for the West, which was far away—a place where a man could lose himself and get a fresh start. Out here, most folks pay you the respect you're due, and they don't ask questions about your past.

"To make a long story short, Traxler made me a proposition. As I said, he wanted to start his own business, and he wanted a front man—someone who would pose as the owner while he remained in the background and made the real decisions. Obviously, a man with a large sum of capital draws quite a bit of attention. If his family ever did make inquiries—even as far away as St. Jo—I would be the man toward whom the inquiries would be directed. He would be in the background. He offered me a handsome salary. I don't mind telling you that the offer appealed to me, and I quickly accepted. We became partners—of a sort. Shortly after his arrival here, he began to make a number of purchases—a hotel, a freight line, a home. He was financially active, and he prospered. Of course, he relied on my skills and frequently took my advice on matters of investments— but I was the bookkeeper. He was the one who pulled all the strings. I was able to live in a nice room in his house, and I enjoyed staying in a suite in his hotel when I occasioned to spend the night in town.

"He did have a deep fear of private inquiry agents. On more than one occasion, he made reference to the Pinkertons. He was moody and frequently retired to his room for days at a time. There were periods when he visited that cabin in the bog, where no one went. I believe that that was the only place where he truly felt secure.

"Even as a frontman, I was cautioned to stay out of the public eye as much as possible. I explained to him that such an arrangement might work for a time, but that it could not go on forever. He agreed, but he was determined to live in this fashion until he felt that his family was either unable to locate him or had given up the search. He thought that after a year or two, he would be able to step out of the shadows. It seemed reasonable to me at the time, and I had no reason to question his story. During our relationship, he never broke the law as far as I could tell. I did hear disturbing rumors about some of the men he hired to run his freight line. Lynch, for example, was a man I never trusted, but then men in that line of work can be rough around the edges. Besides, I never had much contact with him or the other employees for that matter—I was just a paper and pencil man.

"For the first time, I truly suspected that there was something seriously wrong two days ago. I overheard only bits and pieces of conversation between Traxler and Lynch, but I felt something ominous in the air. I heard Lynch issue orders to some of the men— something about the old relay station, but I had no idea what was going on. I also heard something about a woman—Miss Stuart as it turned out." He turned toward Waverly, Chandler, and Connors. "The deputy here told me a little about Traxler's background. I was shocked to hear about his involvement with you . . . of what he did to you. I'm just sorry that it ever had to happen."

Waverly nodded.

Storm climbed to his feet and walked around to the front of the desk. "Well, Mr. Ludlow, from what you told me, I don't think we'll be needin' you for anything else at this time. There will be reports and statements that will have to be signed. I'll send for you when the time comes."

"Then, you're not going to hold me?"

"No, sir. It looks as though you were taken in by this man same as the rest of the folks in St. Jo."

"What happens to the businesses now, Deputy—the hotel, the freight line . . . my position?" Ludlow asked.

"I'll be contacting the federal authorities. They'll have to sort things out. Could take some time. You might as well just stay on and continue to run things until matters are set right."

Ludlow nodded. "All right. I'll do that. I've saved some money. Maybe I can make a deal to buy an interest in the hotel, at least. There's no reason why a going concern shouldn't continue."

"I agree," Storm said.

Ludlow stood and straightened his coat. "Gentlemen," he said and then turned and left.

"Well, that explains quite a bit," Storm said.

"It confirms what Traxler did with the money that we buried," Chandler returned.

Storm poured himself some coffee from a pot that rested on an old black stove. "I'll expect you boys to stay in town for a while. The sheriff will want to meet you after I give him the story of what happened. I'm sure there'll be government officials comin' to St. Jo as well, and they'll have questions for you."

"We'll be around for a while," Waverly replied.

"Fine. I appreciate you comin' in."

They left the jailhouse and meandered out onto the boardwalk, where they stood for some time without talking as they simply studied the traffic on the street. Finally, Waverly said, "Well, Dell, what plans do you and Marion have?"

Chandler pushed back his Stetson. "We talked about staying in St. Jo for a while. I thought that we might take a room at one of the hotels . . . try to adjust to being together again."

"Sounds good. I'm glad that I got to meet Marion. She seems like a fine woman. I hope that things work out for you," Waverly said.

"She is, and thanks, Captain."

"Me . . . I'm seriously considering going into the

freight business on a permanent basis," Connors announced. "Orrin is kind of young. He could use the guidance of a more experienced man."

"Like you, eh?"

"Can you think of a better man?" Connors grinned.

"No, I truly can't," Waverly returned with a smile.

There was a long pause as Chandler and Connors regarded Waverly. They glanced at each other, and then Connors asked, "And you, Captain . . . you've found something here as well, haven't you?"

Waverly gazed down the street in the direction of Stuart's freight office. "I wonder if Nora is in her office yet? I think I'll ask her to dinner this evening."

Chandler and Connors grinned at each other as Waverly made his way down the boardwalk.

Waverly was lost with his thoughts as he walked slowly toward the freight office. He hesitated as he took hold of the doorknob, but he finally turned it and walked in.

Nora was standing behind the counter. She looked up as Waverly entered. She seemed edgy, apprehensive. "Hello, John. Did you get matters straightened out with Joe Storm?"

Waverly nodded. "Carl Ludlow told us about his true relationship with Traxler. He was cooperative. It looks as though he was deceived by Traxler as well as many others."

"What will happen now?"

"Federal authorities will conduct an investigation. More than likely, they will try to recover the money that Traxler stole. His business interests will be targeted."

"That could take a long time."

"Most likely."

Nora avoided eye contact with Waverly as she glanced over the ledger in front of her.

Waverly rested his hands on the counter. "Nora, the real reason I came by was to ask you to dinner this evening."

Nora's eyes widened as she looked up. "John, I'd like that."

"It appears as though we may be here in St. Jo for a while."

"What about California?"

"It will always be there, but then, I don't know anyone in California. Besides, it's a long ride to find something that I may have already found right here."

B